STAR

of

WONDER

a sweet Victorian holiday novella

K. LYN SMITH

Star of Wonder is a work of fiction. Unless otherwise indicated,
names, characters, places and incidents are products of the
author's imagination, or are used fictitiously. Any resemblance
to actual events, locales or persons, living or dead, is entirely
coincidental.

Davenwood Press, USA
ISBN: 979-8-9911573-1-5

"Love knows not distance;
it hath no continent;
its eyes are for the stars."

– Gilbert Parker

CHAPTER ONE

LETTER FROM ANDREW GREY to Miss Aster Corbyn, crumpled and dashed upon Miss Corbyn's hearth then hastily retrieved and smoothed upon her desk:

8th January 1839
Cavalry Barracks, Hounslow, London

Dear Aster,

I realize not more than forty-eight hours have passed since I left you in Kent, but I write to fulfill my promise to keep you apprised of my situation (insomuch as my post allows). My post. The words make me smile, and I can hardly believe I've been so "utterly beef-witted" (as you succinctly put it) to cast my lot with Her Majesty's finest, although you have to admit, the scarlet coat does lend a certain dash. My incredulity is matched only by yours, I suspect. And possibly that of my parents.

At any rate, my company remains in England until the end of February, so you see, we're not so distant from one another yet. Keep watch on our star and I shall do the same.

Yours,
A

—

REPLY FROM MISS ASTER CORBYN to Andrew Grey, tear-stained:

10th January 1839
Redstone Hall, Kent

Dear Andrew,
I stand by my earlier assessment: you are an utter beef-wit to leave me so unexpectedly (although I reluctantly thank you for your diligence in keeping me apprised of your situation). Your mother's eyes grew suspiciously damp when I mentioned your name at tea, and I harbor only the tiniest bit of guilt in bringing it to your attention.

Not so fondly,
A

—

LETTER FROM ANDREW GREY to Miss Aster Corbyn, also crumpled and flung upon Miss Corbyn's hearth before being tucked into her writing desk:

29th January 1839
Cavalry Barracks, Hounslow, London

Dear Aster,

I write with exciting news: our departure has been accelerated. By the time you receive this, I will have sailed for India. I've had occasion to speak with a number of fellow soldiers who have returned from that exotic land, and my enthusiasm only grows for the adventure that awaits. Worry not; I shall write and share all the details.

Have you returned to London yet for the new term? I'm certain your teaching post will keep you so thoroughly occupied you'll hardly know I've gone.

Indeed, the months will fly and before you know it, we shall see one another again.

Yours,
A

PS: Never say you're still put out with me. I couldn't bear the loss of my Faster Aster's affection.

—

REPLY FROM MISS ASTER CORBYN to Andrew Grey, also tear-stained:

31st January 1839
Mrs. Ivy's School for Girls, London

Dear Andrew,

You've truly gone then? I am still put out with you, but as you say, my teaching post does keep me quite busy. So much so that I hardly have time to think of you at all. Despite this (and in case you're unable to decipher the true nature of my feelings), I miss you dreadfully. Your smile and your laughter make my heart sing. Ironically, England is greyer with one less Grey. Please return safely, and soon.

Your friend,
A

—

LETTER FROM ANDREW GREY to Miss Aster Corbyn, stained a questionable shade of brown:

30th June 1840
Custom-House, Calcutta, India

Dear Aster,

We depart Calcutta soon and journey to Cawnpore, which is seven hundred and fifty miles distant. I'm told that's more than the entire distance from the northern tip of Scotland to the southern coast of our fair country, although it spans but a mere fraction of this land. We're to travel by way of the Hooghly and Ganges rivers over the course of fourteen days. I believe that equates to a rate of fifty-four miles per day. (You may confirm and correct my calculation if need be. I suspect you will have already done so by this point.)

Thank you for sending the chart, so I might find our star in this unfamiliar sky. I continue to watch it and am comforted to think of you doing the same.

Yours,

A

PS: Please excuse the coffee stains. My companion, Lieutenant Monty Doyle, is not the tidiest of bunk mates.

———

LETTER FROM MISS ASTER CORBYN to Captain Andrew Grey:

5th December 1841
Redstone Hall, Kent

Dear Andrew,

I can hardly fathom you've been gone for nearly two years. I write from Redstone Hall, where I've returned to spend Christmastide with my family. My parents and sisters arrived two days ago, and my brother Edmund came down from school only this afternoon. I know you would be amazed at how much he's grown!

Today, of course, is the eve of St. Nicholas, and as always, there is an air of excitement about the Hall that is unique to this time of year. (Never mind that all of us are too old to believe any longer in the "magic" that brings sweets and coins to our shoes while we sleep. My father must persist in perpetuating the myth and we persist in indulging him.)

You have my congratulations on your well-deserved promotion to the rank of Captain. Although, if you've gained it in the same manner in which you achieved your supposed victories in our childhood games . . . Well, I shall say no more on that subject.

It relieves me to know you're safely arrived in Bombay; your account of the perils along your journey lifted the hairs on the back of my neck. I continue to watch our star and pray for your safety, if no longer your swift return.

Your friend,
A

CHAPTER TWO

BOMBAY
MAY 1844

Andrew stifled a groan as the doctor left his bedside to tend the rest of his patients. The stench of blood was sickening and inescapable, and he feared he might embarrass himself once again. He swallowed back the bile in his throat.

A man moaned to his left. He imagined most of the fellows to either side of him had been attacked by tigers (in the plural) or run through with the tip of an enemy's blade. Certainly, none had been so beef-witted to mangle themselves on a *tree*.

Sweat beaded his lip and fever burned his brow, but none of that was anything to the lance stabbing his leg.

Dr. Heyworth couldn't have any more years than

Andrew's own two and twenty. The fellow seemed tolerably well versed in general anatomy, but he certainly couldn't boast the expertise or experience of Andrew's physician father or his surgeon mother. Certainly, he inspired neither trust nor confidence. Why, the man's hand had *trembled* as he'd inspected the torn flesh of Andrew's thigh, and Andrew had found only marginal comfort in the presence of an older gentleman at Heyworth's elbow, a mentor of sorts.

"Be sure to leave enough skin to cover the stump," the mentor had said. Heyworth nodded uncertainly at this counsel before leaving Andrew to his rampaging thoughts.

He squeezed his eyes shut. When he opened them again, the shadow of Montgomery Doyle darkened his narrow cot. Monty removed the cheroot from between his lips and frowned.

"Ye have to be the most fortunate man I've ever had the, er, misfortune to meet, Captain. We all thought ye were done for when the cliff fell away."

"King?" Andrew's voice was a rough croak that sounded nothing like him.

"Your horse is fine," Monty said, his Irish brogue making *horse* sound like *arse*. "It took some doin', but with ropes and patience, he was fished up."

Andrew nodded. That was some small comfort. Their company had traveled a good distance from their planned route so they might cross the rain-swollen Godavari. King had confidently picked his way along the edge of a precipice until the sodden ground gave way beneath his hind legs. His mount had made several honorable attempts with his fore feet before falling backwards, and Andrew had awakened some thirty feet below, wedged in a thorny tree without any recollection of how he'd got there. His horse, to his relieved surprise, had been stopped by another tree some fifteen paces further below.

Monty snuffed his cheroot on the floor before adding, "Ye were not so easy to fetch up. Of the two of ye, I'd say your horse was the more agreeable to our noble efforts on your behalf."

Andrew scowled at his friend and tried to call up a suitably sarcastic retort, but the effort died beneath the agony-tinged haze fogging his brain.

Monty reached into his coat and extracted a stack of letters. "I retrieved your post, by the by," he said. "Ye've received a few letters from England. These"—he squinted—"are difficult to decipher, but the frank is from London."

His mother. Her penmanship had always been abysmal.

"But this one has promise. The script is neat and precise. It's definitely in a lady's hand." Monty lifted the missive to his nose and sniffed. "'Tis a pity the crossin' is so long. I imagine it must've smelled nice once."

Aster. Andrew closed his eyes again. Even without the scent on the letter he could still recall her soft, lemony fragrance.

She'd written him faithfully for five years. He'd considered cashing out and returning to her—many, many times—but he wasn't ready. He wasn't the man she deserved yet. And now, with his leg wrapped in blood-soaked linens, he was even further from his aim.

"Would ye like me to read it to ye?" Monty asked with an eager waggle of his woolly brows.

"No," Andrew grumbled as a rivulet of sweat slicked down his cheek. His whole body was afire, heat radiating from his leg to his fingertips. Even his eyelashes felt hot. He reached within himself for the devil-may-care attitude he was known for, but it eluded him.

His insouciance had seen him safely through his twenty-two years—up to this point, at any rate. As a boy, it had poked and teased at Aster until she held her sides with laughter. And then, it had made the years of separation from her bearable.

But now, that character was so distant from him as to be another person entirely. In his delirium, he saw himself shriveling into an embittered and humorless man with naught more than a stump for a leg. *That* was not the man for Aster.

And that was enough of a rallying cry to bring him back to himself.

"Monty," he grunted. "Don't let them take my leg."

His friend's thick brows lifted before collapsing across the bridge of his nose. Monty lowered his voice to say, "The sawbones says there's nothin' to be done. If they don't take the leg, it'll fester and ye'll probably die."

"Probably?" Probably was not certainly.

"Ye'll die, Grey."

"Don't let them take the leg, Monty. If you allow it, I'll retrieve it from the rubbish bin and beat you about the head with it."

—

Letter from Miss Aster Corbyn to Captain Andrew Grey:

1st June 1844
Mrs. Ivy's School for Girls, London

Dear Andrew,

It's been some months since my last letter and I've yet to receive your reply. I hope you are well and haven't been so jingle-brained as to get yourself ~~married~~ shot. You know how much I would be put out with you if that were the case. Please write as soon as you are able and let me know how you fare. I know your family is eager for news of you as well.

Your friend,
A

—

LETTER FROM ANDREW GREY to Miss Aster Corbyn:

3rd September 1844
Bombay, India

Dear Aster,

Never fear for me; I remain hale and hearty, albeit soggy beneath these infernal rains. It will be nice to dry out soon. How I envy your London summer, which is absolutely arid by comparison.

Did I tell you about the time our company was thwarted by the floodwaters north of Bombay? They necessitated we travel ten miles off our route until we could locate a point of safe crossing.

I was dismayed to lose my pocket watch on that journey; you'll recall, it was the one I acquired from the jeweler in Marshfield on the occasion of my sixteenth birthday. Until its loss, I never passed a day without it. Not only did it remind me of the last harvest festival we enjoyed together, but you said it (finally) made me appear a man of some consequence. Now, I fear I'm not only lighter of pocket and perpetually late, but inconsequential, to boot.

Yours (of less consequence),
A

———

LETTER FROM MISS ASTER CORBYN to Captain Andrew Grey, sent but never received:

5th December 1844
Mrs. Ivy's School for Girls, London

Dear Andrew,

I was relieved to learn of your continued existence but dismayed to hear of the loss of your watch. I'm certain when next we meet, you will have quite fallen in my esteem without its dignity to hold you up.

And now I have a serious question to put to you, and I beg you will set aside your merry grin for a moment. (Yes, even now, I can picture it.) It has been some years since you left for India, and even more that we have called one another friend.

My question to you is this: do you still feel as fondly for me as you once did? I don't hold it against you if your sentiment has changed, but I should like to know if there will ever be more for us than letters across these vast oceans. Please don't leave me in suspense.

Always your friend,
A

PS: Regardless of your response to my question, I have a gift for you. I shan't send it on but shall carry it about with me as an encouragement for your safe return.

CHAPTER THREE

MARCH 1845

ANDREW FROWNED AT THE UNOPENED letter in his hand then turned to his friend in consternation. "This is all?"

Monty nodded. "Ye were expecting somethin' more? Per'aps a letter from a certain lady with tidy penmanship? I'm sorry, m'friend."

Andrew limped to the window, his cane thumping the wood floor. He turned the letter in his hand, noting his mother's messy scrawl. Perhaps she'd sent news of Aster. It wasn't like his friend to go so long without writing. She'd *always* made an effort to write to him at the holiday.

"Might I suggest ye inform the lady of your change in circumstance . . ." Monty's voice trailed off at Andrew's scowl, and he held his hands up. This was ground they'd previously crossed. "Ah, forget I mentioned it," Monty said.

He took up his hat to leave, but Andrew's mind had already dismissed his friend. Had Aster lost interest in their correspondence? In him? No, he couldn't—wouldn't—imagine it. The mail was ridiculously unreliable and while Monty was the best of friends, he wasn't always the most diligent errand boy. Perhaps he'd missed a letter somewhere.

He stared at the gardens below for some minutes then thumped back to his desk. Tossing his cane aside, he retrieved a fresh sheet of paper.

He wrote letter after letter, each more desperate than the last. There was simply no way to inquire if she still cared for him without the words casting a pall of forlorn anxiety over the missive. Finally, he stopped, head in his hands. A sea of crumpled pages littered the floor beneath him.

In the end, he wrote to her of General Thurston's ball, held Friday last. It was an entertaining account—quite rollicking, in fact—and he smiled to think of her laughter as she read it.

—

LETTER FROM MISS ASTER CORBYN to Captain Andrew Grey; unsent, crumpled and tossed upon Miss Corbyn's hearth:

1st July 1845
Redstone Hall, Kent

Dear Andrew,

I was sorry (and somewhat surprised) to hear the curry at the general's ball didn't agree with you, as you have always had an intrepid appetite.

And now, I have a bit of news of my own. I'm to be married. I know; it quite confounds the mind, doesn't it? Papa wishes me to wait until after the new year, but I believe the months will fly.

Always your friend,
A

——

LETTER FROM MISS HELEN CORBYN to Captain Andrew Grey, with enclosure:

2nd July 1845
Redstone Hall, Kent

Dear Andrew,

I've no doubt you will be surprised (alarmed, even) to receive a letter from me, as we've not had occasion to correspond since you left England more than Six Years Ago.

Do not concern yourself as everyone here is safe and healthy. However, I found the enclosed letter in my sister's ~~fireplace~~ room and consider it my duty to see it properly delivered. I'm certain it was merely by oversight that Aster neglected to frank it to you, just as I am confident you will find her news of interest.

Sincerely,
Miss Helen Corbyn

PS: May I suggest you not disclose the source of this information?

2nd PS: I, too, was sorry to learn the curry at the general's ball did not agree with you, but then, I've often told Aster you are bold as brass. To which comments she has stoutly and most consistently defended you.

—

MARRIED? ANDREW TURNED THE PAGES over, but there was no more on the matter. Neither Aster nor her sister had offered further details of the fellow who'd captured Aster's interest. His name, his age, his occupation. Did the man even have an occupation, or was he some idle lordling? He couldn't see Aster abiding idleness.

He rubbed the scar on his leg through his linen

trousers. Across his tidy bungalow, trunks were stacked and piled with silks and cashmere, spices and tea. He'd thought to leave India long before now. Had, in fact, planned to send for the silk-turbaned porters to load his belongings onto a cart and then onto a ship. But one distraction had led to another, and despite the prize he'd hoped awaited him in England, he'd not been able to muster himself to the port.

But now, it seemed, the prize that had encouraged him through monsoons and marauders, hunger and heat, illness and injury, was no longer his to claim.

No. He wouldn't think it. Aster could not be lost to him.

He took out a clean sheet of paper, addressed it to Aster and wrote, *Married?* His breath came fast and heavily through his nose until his head grew fuzzy. The pen splattered ink across the page where he dropped it, obscuring the single word. Married.

—

LETTER FROM ANDREW GREY to his mother, Mrs. Julian Grey:

10th September 1845
Bombay, India

Dear Mother,

Is it true that Aster Corbyn is to be married? What does Harry Corbyn have to say to such news? I cannot believe he's found a chap worthy of his daughter's affections.

Don't trouble yourself with a reply. It won't reach me in Bombay as I have some news of my own. I'm returning to England. I expect to arrive at Fernwood at the start of Advent or soon thereafter. I look forward to seeing you and Father.

All my best, etc.
Andrew

CHAPTER FOUR

LONDON
DECEMBER 1845

ASTER WAVED AS ANOTHER PUPIL departed Mrs. Ivy's School for Girls. Her broad smile was partly for the girls and their parents, but mostly for the fact that it would be Christmas soon and she was returning to Redstone Hall.

Her entire family would be there; she'd never missed a holiday with them, and she couldn't wait to stir the Christmas pudding and hang greenery with her mother and sisters. Watch her father wrestle the Yule log with her brother Edmund.

A fat snowflake landed on her nose, then another. She looked up at the colorless, late-afternoon skies and marveled at the swirling, spinning mass of flakes that had begun to drift earthward.

"Miss Corbyn," a voice said behind her, and she turned to see Mr. Church approaching with his daughter Emily. She smiled. The girl was one of her more promising pupils, who didn't turn her nose up at mathematics.

"I can't wait to hear all about your holiday," Aster said, "and the young gentleman you hope to dance with in Lancashire." This last, she whispered, as she knew Emily would be embarrassed for her father to overhear. A lady should be allowed a *few* secrets at least.

"And I can't wait to"—Emily's face shifted as her father drew near—"learn more of differential geometry."

Aster coughed even as Mr. Church's brows lifted at his daughter's scholastic enthusiasm.

"You'd best hurry, Miss Corbyn, if you wish to catch the last coach," Mrs. Ivy said, coming up on her other side. "This has the makings of the biggest snowfall we've seen in decades. You'll not make it to Kent if you linger."

"I wish you would allow us to drive you," Mr. Church said as he pulled his collar higher against the increasing wind. "You won't reconsider?"

"I thank you, Mr. Church, but I shall be perfectly fine," she assured him. He was beginning to sound like her father, who had repeatedly asked if she wouldn't rather take the train.

Yes, the train would be faster, but it was also noisy, and she'd be covered in coal smoke by the time she reached Marshfield. A train would also require her to converse with other people, and she was looking forward to a quiet journey with only her own thoughts for company. A coach would do just fine.

Mr. Church nodded and adjusted his cuffs. He moved toward his carriage after his daughter then stopped and said, "And the other matter we spoke of . . . You're quite certain?"

Aster smiled at him as a snowflake melted on her cheek. "Yes, Mr. Church. I wish you a happy Christmas."

He nodded and tipped his hat before climbing into the carriage. She watched them ride away as Mrs. Ivy clicked her tongue.

"Such a fine gentleman," she said.

Aster ignored her comment and pulled on her gloves. "Happy Christmas to you, Mrs. Ivy. I shall see you in the new year."

"I look forward to it Miss Corbyn. The girls are excited about their new course of study. Or some of them, rather."

"As am I," Aster said, then she added earnestly, "I'm fully aware of the faith you've placed in me, to allow this expansion of the curriculum. Although, I think the parents' eagerness for it remains to be seen."

"Small steps, Miss Corbyn. Once they realize there's nothing harmful about maths and science they'll come around."

—

IMPATIENCE ATE AT ANDREW'S NORMALLY placid demeanor. He'd had unavoidable business to attend to at East India House and warm clothing to acquire. Those matters had taken days longer than he'd anticipated, but once they'd been dispatched, he pointed his horse toward Kent and gave him his head. At least, insofar as the falling snow permitted. The stuff was growing thicker by the minute; soon he wouldn't be able to see his hand before his face.

It had been an age since he'd had the dubious pleasure of an English winter. The scents of wood and coal smoke lay heavy over London, the air orange with the light of gas lamps shining through the late fog. Nostalgia for such a landscape was unexpected, but it was there nonetheless, just as his eagerness to reach his destination was an ever-present companion.

His stomach twisted with a combination of anxiety and anticipation as he thought of Aster. Would she be pleased to see him, or so eager for her nuptials in the new year that his presence would be little more than a remark over breakfast?

Mama, he imagined her saying, *did you hear that Andrew Grey is returned to England?*

Well, I'm certain his parents must be pleased. Have you given any more thought to your trousseau, dear?

He forced such dark thoughts aside. If he hoped to persuade Aster to abandon this ridiculous notion of marrying someone other than him, he needed to maintain a cheerful outlook.

He stopped at a coaching inn about fifteen miles south of London to change his mount. Carriages clogged the inn's small turnabout, and he maneuvered toward the stables and handed the reins to an ostler. Stomping snow from his boots, he ducked beneath the inn's low lintel and stepped across the threshold.

The air inside was warm, the crowd noisy and the flagstones puddled from snow-dusted travelers. He removed his hat and made for the oak bar and a mug of ale. A group near the fireplace had abandoned their journey in favor of the inn's certain warmth, and laughter rang out among them as a barmaid distributed tall mugs round the table.

A dark blue cloak atop full blue skirts swirled in front of him, and he looked up. Stopped and blinked. Aster.

A slow grin spread across his face. Perhaps the stars favored his quest, for they were surely aligned for him today.

Her face was thinner, her form . . . fuller . . . than he recalled, although it was hard to tell, buttoned up tight as she was from tip to toe. Joy bloomed—there was truly no better word for it—joy *bloomed* within him to see her beloved face.

He recalled her thick, curling hair that had always reminded him of molasses—dark with just a hint of amber in the right light. It barely showed beneath the brim of her bonnet, but he'd have recognized her from her eyes alone. Brilliant and silver, they reminded him of the winking stars she so loved.

He waited for her to recognize him. Her forehead puckered in that delightful way she had when she was thinking. Or irritated. "Andrew?" she whispered.

"'Tis I," he said, making her a pretty bow.

She was silent for a long moment, then her lips twisted to one side. "Well, this is a surprise, indeed. I suppose I should more properly call you Captain Grey. You look well, although I almost didn't recognize you without your scarlet regimentals."

"I can understand your dilemma," he said, "as you've seen me out of them more than in."

A snort of laughter behind him said he'd not kept his voice as low as he'd intended, and the faint coloring on Aster's cheeks said his innuendo had hit home. That he still had the power to bring a blush to her pale skin pleased him to no end, and he wondered if this fiancé of hers could claim as much. His jaw tightened and he forced it to relax.

A grin threatened her stern expression. He waited, breath held, then disappointment winged through him when she conquered it.

"Still incorrigible, I see. Are you traveling to Fernwood?" she asked.

"I am. And you're for Redstone Hall?" At her nod, he continued, "You don't mean to travel there today, do you? The weather grows worse by the hour."

"You're traveling today, are you not?"

"Well, yes, but I'm—" He stopped before he said "a man." "I'm on horseback," he finished.

She gave him a look that said she knew exactly what he'd meant to say. "And I have hired a perfectly sound coach, driven by a perfectly capable coachman."

"Then I shall provide my escort as we're traveling in the same direction. I'll be your *chevalier* to see you safely to your destination." Could his fortune have been any brighter?

"Thank you, Andrew," she said as she adjusted her gloves, "but that's not necessary. My coach, while sound, is slow; I'm afraid we'll only delay your travels, and I'm sure you must be eager to reunite with your family."

"Miss, we'd best be on our way," a roughly dressed man spoke from her side. "I don't like the looks of this weather."

Andrew lifted a brow at her driver's unknowing support, but Aster ignored him.

"Thank you," she nodded at the man. "I'll settle with the innkeeper and be along shortly." To Andrew, she smiled and added, "We'll see one another again soon. I'm certain my parents will have invited your family to Christmas supper."

Her words were brisk and courteous with no hint that she'd affianced herself to another. It was as if she was little more than an acquaintance, not the dearest, deepest friend of his heart. He *was* to be relegated to the breakfast table then.

He frowned and tried to think of something else to say, some way to recapture his place in her heart, but his mind drew up empty. Finally, he nodded and stepped aside to let her pass.

ASTER CAST A SWEEPING GLANCE over her shoulder before stepping into the coach, but she didn't see Andrew anywhere. She adjusted her crinoline and settled onto the seat then pressed a shaking hand to her stomach.

He was home.

Andrew was home.

For years, she'd dreamed of his homecoming. And each imagining went something along the lines of her squealing with delight and him bending to lift her against him. Kissing her madly, passionately, as if he'd never let her go. As if he'd finally realized the utter stupidity of his leaving in the first place. None of which had happened.

Instead, they'd been two near-strangers. *How do you do?* and *Pleasure to see you ma'am. Do you travel to Kent?*

Except for that one bit of ribald teasing. *That* was the incorrigible Andrew she knew, even if the rest of him had seemed so different. Her eyes burned and she blinked rapidly.

He was taller than she remembered, erect with his captain's posture. His dark hair had been lightened and his fair skin darkened by the Indian sun, which he'd explained was nothing like their insipid English sun. When last she'd seen him, dressed proudly in his new regimentals, he'd been a wiry youth, with naught but a promise of strength to come. He'd clearly found it, as his shoulders and chest filled his dark wool coat quite nicely.

He'd returned.

He'd returned, without any word to her of his arrival. That spoke more loudly of his intentions where she was concerned than any letter could have. She inhaled, and the shakiness of her breath irritated her.

Was he married?

Why hadn't she inquired after him?

Have you returned to England alone?

How long will you stay?

What brings you back to England's shores?

She'd not bothered with these or any other questions because she'd fled the coaching inn as quickly as her stays would allow. She'd never been so craven-hearted, but that was before he'd left her behind in favor of the dust and heat and monsoons of India.

Springs creaked and the coach dipped as the driver climbed aboard. Her breath frosted the small windows while snow and ice crusted them from the outside. She resisted the urge to twist in her seat and look for Andrew once more as they pulled away from the inn.

Instead, she curled her hands into her fur muff and moved her feet closer to the warming bricks. Closing her eyes, she focused on the rhythmic rocking of the coach to rescue her from memories that refused to stay down.

CHAPTER FIVE

THE COACH LURCHED VIOLENTLY AND Aster came awake from a dreamless nap, stretching a hand to the cold window to keep from tumbling to the floor. What the bloody—?

They weren't moving. The carriage lay tilted to one side, and the light from the carriage lamps barely penetrated the white frost covering the windows. She reached for the door handle, which was lower than it should have been. Pushing against snow and ice that had frosted the door shut, she nearly tumbled from the carriage when it was wrenched open.

A pair of boots stood in the meager pool of light from the coach lanterns—boots much too fine for her hired coachman. She looked up, and up some more.

"Are you all right?" Andrew asked.

Joy climbed atop her confusion to gain purchase in her mind. She kicked it back down. "Andrew? Where's my coachman?"

"Are you injured?"

"No. Is the coachman all right?"

He blew out a slow breath. "I'm your coachman. And I'm unharmed, thank you for asking."

"What? No, you're not. My coachman, that is. I hired a coachman." She was beginning to sound like a simpleton. She inhaled.

"And I unhired him. Or rather, I acquired his coach and pair."

"You what?" She frowned. "You *bought* the coach?"

"And the horses." She drew a steadying breath, but before she could ask why he would do such a foolish thing, he continued. "Now, if you're uninjured, can I ask you to step out of the coach? We've hit a rut, and I need to get the wheel back on the road."

She shook her head. "Yes. Yes, of course." She gathered her muff and cloak about her and stepped gingerly to the ground. Andrew held her elbow to steady her, and she pulled away from him in irritation. He reached for the top of her mantle, drawing the strings tighter for her, and she batted his hands away.

"Just see to the bloody coach."

"Still a lady, just as I recall."

—

DESPITE THE STARS' EARLIER FAVOR, things were not proceeding as Andrew might have wished. The days were much shorter in England than he recalled. The sky, already gunmetal grey with clouds, had begun to darken with evening, and snow continued to swirl and settle in his lashes. He blinked it away and surveyed the wheel. It rested at an odd angle in a hole about six inches deep. The blowing, drifting snow did a bang-up job disguising the poor road conditions. And, as if that weren't enough of a welcome-home, his leg had begun to ache.

He looked over his shoulder to where Aster stood. Her hands were tucked demurely in her fur muff, but one snow-dusted foot tapped impatiently. He didn't think she was even aware of the movement. She probably thought she was the perfect picture of calm seas.

"I'm going to give the coach a push from behind," he said. "Can you guide the horses?"

She gave a short nod and marched toward the horses' heads.

"It may be best if you climb up on the box and hold the reins," he said. He didn't wish the horses to trample her if the movement at their backs spooked them. She'd always been a good driver; she'd have more certain success holding the reins.

She changed course and eyed the box atop the coach. "I don't think . . . That is, I can't get up there."

He stood and approached her. "Of course you can. Just reach up and take hold here. I can give you a boost if need be."

She tossed an irritated look at him, then when he still didn't comprehend, she lifted her arms out to her sides. They only went as far up as her chest before she dropped them again. Ah. He'd forgotten how restrictive English clothing could be. In India, even the English ladies' seams were somewhat more relaxed, owing to the heat and humidity. He hid his smile; in Aster's present state of mind, any show of levity at this point would only earn him more grief.

"Gather your skirts then," he said with a motion toward her voluminous lower half.

"What?"

"Gather your skirts," he repeated slowly. "I'll hoist you up."

"No, I don't think—Andrew!" She squeaked as he wrapped his arms around her legs and lifted. At least he thought there were legs beneath the bundle in his arms. How many blasted petticoats was she wearing anyway?

"Take hold of the handle there. Can you reach it

now?" His voice was muffled beneath layer upon layer of wool that didn't afford even a hint of what he remembered to be a rather nicely shaped—he stopped that train before it could leave the station.

She fumbled a bit then said breathlessly, "I have it."

"Capital. Now place your foot on the step to your right . . . There."

With a bit more grunting and maneuvering—mostly on his part—she was on the box. She exhaled and adjusted her skirts before beaming her Aster grin on him. Then, untying the reins from where he'd left them, she said, "I'm ready."

He retrieved her muff from where she'd dropped it and tossed it into the coach. Then, moving to the back, he bent and pushed. And pushed some more. Nothing. He turned and tried from another angle, then another as his blasted leg continued to throb. The wind had picked up, and the snow was blowing at him sideways now.

"Are you pushing yet?" she called from atop the box.

"Not yet," he said when he had his breath back.

Finally, he gave one more great shove and—*crack*! The coach listed further to the side.

"What was that?" she said, twisting on the box.

He scrubbed a hand over his face and moved around the coach to the errant wheel.

"Was that the wheel? Did you *break* the wheel?"

He knelt and in the dim light saw the splintered spokes of what had once been a perfectly serviceable wheel.

He wiped the concern from his face and turned to look up at her. "You can come down now," he said.

She fixed the reins then turned to descend from the box. She leaned first one way, then the other as she struggled to bend forward. *Stays.* He knew there was a reason he detested the things. Aside from the fact that they flattened the best parts, that was.

He set his hands on his hips. "You never had this much trouble when we used to climb trees together."

"Yes," she said in her most proper voice—the one that told him she was trying to be a lady although she'd like to peel a strip from him. "I apologize if I didn't come dressed for tree climbing."

"You'll just have to jump. I'll catch you."

"I'm not jumping!" She turned a few more times in an attempt to find a way down that didn't require her to bend at the waist. Finally, seeing the futility of it and acquiescing to his better sense, she sighed and nodded once. "Very well."

He braced himself and held his arms open. She stepped off the box and he caught her to him, taking her weight on his good leg. The brim of her bonnet poked him in the forehead, sending a shower of snowflakes down his face. She hadn't been more than five feet off the ground, but when she and all of her petticoats filled his arms, she took his breath. All of it. He held her to him for a moment, reveling in her soft lemony scent before setting her down slowly.

She couldn't marry this popinjay, whoever he was.

—

ASTER PUSHED AWAY FROM ANDREW and righted her skirts. Her crinoline had become twisted, so she wriggled a bit until the layers fell into proper place again. She drew in a deep breath and released it slowly. Merciful heavens, but Andrew was every bit as hard and broad as he'd appeared in the coaching inn. She followed him to the stuck wheel then gasped at the splintered wood.

"You *did* break it!"

"Well, it certainly wasn't intentional."

"What sort of an—" She paused before she said "idiot." Her father had long predicted her tongue would get the best of her one day. "Who drives into a hole?"

"Have you noticed the inches and inches of snow about?" Andrew waved an arm expansively over the darkening landscape. "I couldn't *see* the hole. And what sort of an idiot undertakes a journey in this weather, anyway? I told you it wasn't safe."

"To which I replied that I have—*had*—a perfectly capable coachman! Who would not have been so bacon-brained to drive us into a *hole*."

Andrew's hands were on his hips, and his chest rose and fell in agitation. Their ragged breathing fogged the air between them, and a snowflake melted on the bridge of his nose and slid to the tip.

"This is solving nothing," he said softly. "We'd best begin walking."

"In this?" She looked about but couldn't see anything beyond a five-foot radius. He moved to unfasten one of the carriage lanterns, and she followed. "Wouldn't it be best to wait for another coach? At least we can remain dry while we do so."

He handed her the lantern and moved to unhitch the horses. "Have you seen any other travelers since we've been here? No one else is foolish enough to attempt a journey in this."

"No one asked you to come. In fact, I distinctly recall saying your escort was not needed."

"Not needed or not wanted?" he asked slowly, and she frowned.

"What difference does it make?"

He scrubbed a hand over his face. "I don't know why you couldn't have simply waited for the weather to pass."

"It's the eve of St. Nicholas," she whispered.

He stopped, head down, hands motionless as he held the traces. "And you've always celebrated with your family."

She nodded. "We've—we've all been busy with our various pursuits. Edmund has his studies, and Eloise is a published author now. And Helen"—her voice caught—"Helen leaves for Africa in the new year. *Africa,*" she finished in wonder. She sniffed back an unexpected tear then jumped when Andrew's thumb appeared to wipe it away. He'd removed his glove, and his hand was warm against her cheek. She resisted the urge to turn her face into it, but only just.

"I'll see you home safely," he said. "It may not be in time to leave your shoes by the window, but I'll see that you're returned to your family."

She released a tense breath and a watery smile. "I know."

His eyes warmed briefly—perhaps due to her trust in him, or perhaps simply because she'd stopped harping at him like a fishwife long enough for him to catch his breath. Or perhaps it was only a trick of the feeble light.

"By my estimation, the next coaching inn will be six miles ahead," he said. "But I saw a cottage less than two miles behind us. A farm of some sort."

He turned back to the horses, surprising her with his brisk efficiency as he finished unhitching them. Then, retrieving his haversack, he swung it over one shoulder. He caught up the reins in one hand and her valise in the other and motioned for her to precede him.

CHAPTER SIX

THEY RETURNED THE WAY THEY'D come until they spied golden lights in the distance. Leaving the road, they crossed broad fields. The snow had grown to a depth of eight or more inches in places, although it was hard to tell with the way the wind swirled the drifts about.

This part of England rarely saw this much snow. Andrew cast a glance upward and mentally shook his fist at the stars that had tempted and teased him with good fortune. Then he concentrated on placing one booted foot before the other as he led the horses behind the light of Aster's lantern.

The hem of her skirt was sodden and crusted with snow, but her back remained straight. Whether that was owing to her stays or her determination was anyone's guess, although he'd suggest a healthy combination of the two.

No, this reunion was most definitely not proceeding as he'd imagined.

Then Aster stumbled. She dropped the lantern and it went out, but not before he saw her land face-first in a thick snow drift. He dropped their bags and the horses' reins and hurried to her, careful not to step on her in the growing darkness.

"Aster! Are you hurt? Is it your ankle?"

Her words were muffled by the snow, but they sounded like "bloody hell." He stroked a hand over her back and asked, "Can you stand?"

"Not while you're on my skirt," she said, turning. She gave a mighty tug and he moved his boot at the same time, and she went sprawling onto her backside, back into the snow.

He ducked his head and held a fist to his mouth.

"I can hear you smiling," she said as she scrambled to stand. He stood with her and bent to dust her off as he'd done countless times when they'd been children. She batted his hands away, and he felt a blush heat his neck to realize how close he'd been to brushing at her stay-flattened curvy bits.

To distract her—and himself—he cleared his throat and asked, "What do they think of your imprudent language at that fancy girls' school?"

He felt her side-eye before she said primly, "Of course, I'm careful of my language in my role as teacher. The girls are very impressionable. You just happen to bring out my . . ."

"Imprudence?"

"My more colorful self."

"Ah. So that's a privilege reserved only for me. I'm honored."

"As you should be." Then she gasped. "Our bags. Where did you drop the bags?"

He turned in the meager light and said, "Don't worry. They're right—" *Crunch.* Something hard and . . . crunchy . . . shifted under his boot, and he felt the weight of her stillness behind him. Then she moaned.

"No. *No, no, no,*" she said as she hurried toward her valise. As she lifted it, he heard glass and metal bits shifting about. It sounded much like a great, heaping pile of coins, although she didn't react as if she'd discovered a treasure. "No," she whispered.

"Aster," he said hesitantly. "I'm sorry. I didn't—" He didn't know what to say. He wasn't sure what could cause her such distress, but he could bear her railing at him much more easily than her forlorn whisper. "I'll replace it, whatever it was that I've broken."

After a sniff, she said, "No, it's all right. It's . . . nothing."

"It didn't sound like 'nothing'," he said tentatively.

"Truly," she said, "it's naught but a . . . an arithmometer."

"A who?"

"An arithmometer—it's, um, a device for adding and subtracting numbers."

Ah. He should have known Aster wouldn't be concerned over a broken comb or perfume bottle. Of course, her most prized item would have to be an arith—whatever she'd called it.

Full darkness had come, and the moon cast little more than a pale, fuzzy light through the falling snow. The air had grown colder, brittle even, with the distinctive scent of snow that he'd forgotten in his years away. He reached a hand for Aster's shoulder, surprised to feel how soggy she was. She would catch her death if they didn't find warm lodgings soon. "Come," he said. He clutched her about the waist and placed her atop one of the horses.

"But there's no saddle," she said, clutching her valise to her.

"Pretend you're a warrior princess in a savage land," he said, lifting the reins. It was a game they'd enjoyed often as children, at her direction, when she'd played the part of an Amazon warrior or a Viking shield-maiden.

"And you're my servant?" she asked.

He could hear the smile in her voice even though he couldn't see it on her face. "Always."

—

ASTER COULDN'T BELIEVE SHE WAS smiling. Here she was in the middle of a blizzard in the middle of nowhere, atop a saddle-less horse, clutching a bag full of broken glass—arithmometer bits, she reminded herself. She was soaked through *all* of her petticoats, and she was *smiling*.

But this was Andrew, and that was his special talent. He'd always been able to make her smile, even when she'd been spotted with fever, or when her father had threatened to lock her in her room for a month *without her books*. That last had never actually come to pass, although she'd probably deserved it for encouraging Eloise to use their mother's paints to "improve" baby Edmund's features.

Andrew's boots crunched ahead of her as he led them through the swirling snow toward twinkling lights in the distance. She was surprised when the lights suddenly materialized into golden windows on a pleasant farmer's cottage. The horses stopped, and Andrew came alongside and gripped her ankle. "I'll speak with the farmer who lives here. I won't be but a moment."

She nodded and watched him approach the cottage's narrow door. Snow-frosted ivy grew over the entry in a great sweeping arch to spread across the stone front of the cottage. The lintels above the windows dripped crystal icicles, and a child's laughter sounded from within.

A short, balding man opened the door at Andrew's knock. They exchanged a moment's conversation, and he looked beyond Andrew's shoulder to where Aster sat atop the horse, wet and bedraggled. He nodded, and after a brief bow, Andrew returned to her.

"Are you limping?" she asked.

"No."

She frowned, certain he'd been limping. "Did you—" she began, but he interrupted before she could finish.

"Mr. Marley says we may stay the night with his family. Go inside and warm yourself, and I'll see to the horses."

"I can help you," she said, rubbing her numb nose.

"You're soaked through, Aster. I'd rather not explain to your father how I allowed you to perish from fever. It won't take me but a moment, and then I'll join you."

The end of his nose was red, as were his cheeks. He stamped his foot, discomfort and impatience evident in his posture. And something else. Something firm and decisive and quite unlike the old Andrew she recalled. She relented with a slow nod.

He reached for her waist and lowered her to the ground, which was a good thing as she couldn't feel her legs any longer. She moved haltingly toward the door of the cottage where a lady waited. Mrs. Marley, she presumed.

"Oh, and Aster?" Andrew said from her side.

"Yes?"

He leaned down to whisper. "You're the lovely Mrs. Grey tonight."

—

AND THAT, ASTER THOUGHT IN irritation as she watched him lead the horses away, was the old Andrew once again.

"Oh, you poor dear," Mrs. Marley exclaimed. "Your husband told Mr. Marley of your misfortune, and you in a delicate condition, no less. You must be near to frozen through."

Aster's lips flattened into a thin line, then she forced a smile for Mrs. Marley's benefit. "We thank you for opening your home to us, ma'am. I'm afraid Captain Grey's driving ability isn't what it once was. Ever since his head injury . . ."

"Oh, my. Well, come inside and warm yourself by the fire."

Mrs. Marley wore a dark brown dress that matched a tiny mole on her cheek. Her eyes were kind, her voice soft as she fluttered about. The Marley cottage was tidy, with worn wood-planked floors, whitewashed walls, and rooms flanking either side of the narrow entry.

"Don't you worry about a thing," Mrs. Marley said. "We'll have you and your captain dry and snug in no time."

Aster followed her to a warm parlor where a fire burned merrily in the grate. Five children of varying ages looked up, and she assumed her best teacher smile.

"Good evening," she said.

"Are you Mary?" one boy—the youngest—asked. "Come to seek shelter for the birth of baby Jesus?"

"Oh, hush Daniel," Mrs. Marley said. "Pay him no mind," she said to Aster. "He's been practicing for the vicar's nativity."

Aster smiled at Daniel. "No, I'm not Mary," she said. "You may call me Aster."

"Like the flower?" one of the girls asked.

"Well, yes, but 'Aster' also means 'star.' My father is an astronomer, you see."

"Now, you children know your manners. She's Mrs. Grey to you."

"What's an ast—astromer?"

"An astronomer. It's someone who studies the stars and planets." She smiled to think what her father would make of that oversimplified definition. She'd effectively reduced decades of his work and study to one sentence.

"You must be hungry," Mrs. Marley said. "I was putting a stew on the fire when you arrived. Come, girls," she directed her daughters. "You can finish with the carrots."

"I'll assist you," Aster said in a rush. By her count, the Marleys had seven mouths to feed and now two more besides. She hoped their arrival wouldn't strain the Marley purse.

"And I'll gladly accept the help," Mrs. Marley said, "but only after you've changed into some dry clothing. Come, I've some things that might fit you. They're not so grand as what you may be used to, I'm sure, but they're dry and clean."

—

Mr. Marley showed Andrew to a small bedroom upstairs where he could leave their bags and hang his coat to dry.

"My oldest two will bed down with the younger ones tonight, and you and your missus can have this room."

Andrew swallowed and nodded. He'd suspected that, given the relative size of the Marley brood compared to the Marley cottage, he and Aster would need to share accommodations (hence, their sudden "marriage"). But the reality of their sleeping arrangements left him a bit dry-mouthed.

Mr. Marley left him, and he entered to find Aster's blue dress hung to dry near the fire, along with a chemise and petticoat. And another petticoat. *Aaand* her stays.

He approached the fireplace and draped his own coat across a chair. He tried to avoid looking too closely at Aster's things, but he couldn't help being intrigued. He'd seen a lady's underthings before, but these were *Aster's*. They'd been pressed to her skin. He imagined he could smell her warm, lemony scent rising from the drying linen. He ran a fingertip gently along the edge of her stays.

A noise at the door had him dropping his hand from the cookie jar, so to speak, and spinning. A small, tow-headed boy peeked around the corner of the door post, and his breathing relaxed. He didn't imagine Aster would appreciate him handling her personal bits, despite the years of their acquaintance. She'd probably box his ears if she caught him.

The boy disappeared, small feet thumping down the hall, and Andrew took in the rest of the room.

A heavy wool curtain made an admirable attempt to bar the chill wind that whistled along the edge of a small window. There was a small vanity and a thick, woven rug. A narrow wardrobe opposite a bed barely large enough for one. He swallowed around the tightness in his throat then quickly dropped their bags near the hearth, wincing at the rattle of broken bits in Aster's valise.

He untied his haversack, checking for the small leather pouch he'd tied to the inside. Relieved to feel its small weight, he left to join the others below stairs.

CHAPTER SEVEN

ASTER HELD HER BREATH AND listened to the stillness. He didn't make a sound, but she knew Andrew was awake. It was unlikely either of them would find sleep this night.

She considered reading. She reached for the book she'd tucked under her pillow, but she suspected even Mr. Babbage's *On the Influence of Signs in Mathematical Reasoning* wouldn't hold her interest tonight.

The moon had turned the wintry landscape beyond the small window an otherworldly blue. She lay atop the small bed, fully dressed down to her borrowed stays and petticoats, although she'd left her boots to dry by the fire. Her stockinged feet hung off the end of the short bed, extended some three inches below Mrs. Marley's too-short dress. The lady had a preference for brown, but she'd been correct: the dress was warm and dry, and Aster was grateful for it.

When she'd learned that she and Andrew would share the room, her cheeks had ignited to think of her underthings laid out before the fire. As soon as she'd been able, she'd escaped the kitchen, taken the garments down and hastily tucked them in the bottom of the wardrobe. Even now, her face warmed more than the low fire warranted.

Now, Andrew was stretched across the woven rug to take up most of the floor space, his now-dry coat rolled beneath his head as a pillow. She winced to think of him on the cold, hard floor. He couldn't be comfortable, but he assured her he'd passed many a night camping on naught but hard Indian earth. A woven rug would be a luxury, to hear him tell it.

Despite the low fire, the room was cold, and she shivered. Her toes felt like tiny chips of ice in her grey woolen stockings, but she resisted the urge to climb beneath the quilts. There was something unutterably intimate about being *in* the bed versus *on* the bed. That was probably a line they shouldn't cross. Although, in truth, they'd crossed a good many today . . .

She felt his sigh in the silence, although he didn't make a sound.

"What?" she asked, giving up all pretense of sleep.

He was silent for a moment longer before saying, "Your father's going to disembowel me."

She smiled in the flickering light of the fire. "Probably."

"Then he'll flay me. There will be naught but bones left when he's finished."

"I imagine so."

A long silence stretched between them, then he said, "It will be worth it." He shifted his coat-pillow and turned toward the fire, leaving her to stare at the ceiling.

He'd never even acknowledged her last letter — the one where she'd inquired as to the depth of his sentiment — nor had he given any indication that he recalled the promises they'd once exchanged. And now he had the audacity to drop something like *that* into the air between them?

He couldn't leave her with such a statement and then go to *sleep*. She tossed her pillow at his head, perhaps with a little more force than necessary.

"What?" he mumbled, replacing his coat with her pillow.

She leaned on her elbow and stared at his back. "What did you mean by that?"

"Go to sleep, Faster Aster."

She frowned at him, but the effort was wasted on his back as he continued to face the fireplace.

"I can hear you frowning," he said.

"No one calls me that ridiculous name anymore. And don't think to distract me. What did you mean by that remark? What's worth it?"

He sighed and tossed words carelessly over his shoulder. "I meant only that, if I must die a horrible, bloody death at the end of your father's pencil or whatever, it's worth it to spend my last few hours with a dear friend."

His *friend*. Of course. She should have known she'd always, only, ever been his friend. Her stomach shifted with a warm, uncomfortable twist. She sank back down on the bed and stared at the ceiling again. "May I have my pillow, please?"

"No."

The silence stretched and lengthened as the fire threw tall shadows to dance upon the short walls. "Then will you tell me about India?"

He shifted and turned to face her, pausing dramatically to plump her pillow. Then, settling once more, he began. "It's hotter than a . . . Suffice to say, it's hot. And damp, but not England-damp. India-damp is like nothing you've ever felt before. When the monsoon arrives in Bombay . . ."

He whispered tales from his years there—of the monsoon rains but also of exotic foods and animals, the prose and verse of the Maratha, his colonel and fellow soldiers. Much of which he'd already told her in his letters, but she smiled at the retelling, to hear his days recounted in his own voice.

Lord, she'd missed his voice.

—

ANDREW'S WORDS TRAILED OFF AND he listened to Aster's slow, even breathing. He'd loved sharing his stories of India with her, but they'd been bittersweet as well. Because with each adventure, with each trial that he'd experienced over the years, he'd longed to have her there by his side, not months and oceans away.

But India was no place for a gently bred English lady. He'd conveniently argued this to himself time and time again, even as he'd dined with his colonel and his colonel's wife or greeted his friends' wives in the bazaar.

The truth of the matter, when he allowed himself to think on it, was this: Aster was surrounded by *greatness.*

Her father was an astronomer and quite well respected in his field. Her mother, Lady Celeste, was an extraordinary artist who frequently exhibited her paintings at the Royal Academy, and her siblings demonstrated the same unfortunate tendency to exceed all expectations set for them. Andrew couldn't compete with such distinction for a place in Aster's heart.

He'd never ask her to choose between her illustrious family and his poor self, much less follow him halfway round the world. Not until he made something of himself. Not until he was certain she'd choose *him*.

Now, he wondered if her absent fiancé would be so considerate. Was he a man of some renown, or did he expect Aster to settle for mediocrity?

He rubbed the whiskers along his jaw, certain Aster would not align herself with mediocrity. She hadn't earned the name Faster Aster for nothing.

He'd given her the moniker when they'd been children, and it had stuck. She'd always striven to be faster, taller, bigger, better than anyone. Whether they were doing sums or climbing trees, she had a competitive nature unlike any he'd ever seen, before or since. Sometimes it was enough to overwhelm a man, but more often than not, it simply filled him with joy. *She* filled him with joy.

Then he wondered why, as they'd discussed his imminent disembowelment at her father's hand, she'd not once mentioned her beau. As angry as her father would be over their shared accommodations, he imagined a betrothed suitor might be a tad more distressed. He certainly would have been.

CHAPTER EIGHT

ASTER WOKE TO THE CHEERFUL sound of popping logs. She opened her eyes slowly. The room was still cast in semi-darkness, but the fire had been stoked and burned merrily in the grate. A log settled, sending a shower of sparks up the chimney. She sighed and snuggled deeper into the warmth of the quilt—The quilt?

Her eyes flew open again, and she studied the dark wool clenched in her hand. It wasn't Mrs. Marley's quilt but Andrew's coat wrapped about her.

Andrew. He'd come home.

She looked to the floor, but his rug was empty. Reaching a hand behind her, she felt the plump, downy softness of the pillow beneath her head.

Before she could stop herself, she inhaled, taking in a noseful of his cologne from the wool of his coat. It was unfamiliar, as much of him was to her now.

Soft and spicy and slightly exotic, it didn't align with the uncomplicated Andrew she'd known years before.

She cast her gaze about the rest of the room, noting his comb and tin of cinnamon tooth powder on the vanity. Her dress, now dry, hung on a peg by the door, and a tidy pile of linen rested atop Andrew's haversack. His shirt from the day before, folded with soldier-square precision. She blushed to think of him exchanging it for a fresh one, even as she wondered how he'd got the corners so crisp.

The sky beyond the window was still dark, the wind softened to a low whisper as the first faint stirrings of the household reached her. She reluctantly climbed from the depths of Andrew's warm wool and folded his coat, although, to her irritation, her valeting skills were not nearly a match for his.

She retrieved her stays and crinoline from the bottom of the wardrobe, and Kitty, the eldest Marley girl, helped do up her laces. The younger girls followed their sister into the room and exclaimed over the bounty discovered in their shoes that morning.

To Aster's delight, the Marleys celebrated St. Nicholas's Day much like her own family. The children had made much ado about the placement of their shoes before the parlor window the previous night, and by the sound of the girls' excited chatter behind her, their careful consideration had paid dividends.

"Mine had more sweets than Elsie's," Betsy claimed.

"It did not!"

"It did," Betsy said solemnly as Kitty, who was too old for such childish concerns, rolled her eyes at Aster.

Regardless of who had received the greater number of sweets, the girls agreed the biggest surprise had been the shiny coin found in each shoe.

"St. Nicholas has never left us coins before," Elsie whispered.

Properly trussed in her own garments once more, Aster moved to the small vanity to make some sense of her hair. She unwound her plait and pulled a brush through the tangles before twisting the mass into a knot at the back of her head.

"Oh, Mrs. Grey!" Betsy exclaimed as Aster applied her pins. "St. Nicholas has paid you a visit too!"

Aster turned to her in confusion, arms suspended at the back of her head. Betsy stood before the hearth and stared at Aster's boots as the other girls gathered around her.

"Oooh, he has!" Elsie said. "Although I don't know where you'll spend a funny coin like that.

Maybe he's left you a sweet or two in the toe."

Aster shoved in the last pin and joined the girls. They were correct. There, nestled in her boot, lay a shiny gold . . . rupee.

Andrew.

Tears clogged her throat even as a smile threatened her lips. Foreign cologne aside, this was the Andrew she knew. He was forever doing little, thoughtful acts. Covering her with his quilt. Returning her pillow. Leaving a rupee in her boot. It was his way of ensuring no one stayed angry with him for long, but it didn't change the fact that, in all the years she'd known him, the *one thing* she'd needed him to do, he'd been unable to. Or unwilling.

Unable or unwilling, it didn't matter as the end result was the same.

He'd not loved her enough to stay.

—

A WINTRY LANDSCAPE APPEARED BY slow degrees with the rising sun. The snow had continued well into the night, and the wind had cast it about to form tall drifts against trees and ditches and walls. Andrew, accompanied by Mr. Marley and bundled to his eyes in wool, opened the entry door to find a tower of the white stuff banked against the cottage.

What he wouldn't give for a proper southwesterly monsoon.

A gasp on the stairs had him turning to see Aster, one pale hand pressed to her throat as she stared at their snowy fortress. Worried grey eyes flew to his and he crossed to her. He pulled down the scarf covering his face and said, "It doesn't appear we're going anywhere today. Even once we dig our way out, the roads will be impassable, at least until some of the snow melts."

She nodded uncertainly as she gazed at the winter landscape beyond the cottage windows.

"This is southern England," he said, as if she needed reminding. "It will melt soon. Another day or two at worst."

Her eyes widened. "My parents will be worried. They were expecting me"—she hesitated and glanced at the Marleys gathered nearby—"they were expecting *us* last night."

Her eyes were luminous. Aster wasn't a weepy female, but he hurried to say, "They know you— we—couldn't have continued on in this. They'll assume we took lodgings until the roads improve." He leaned closer to whisper, "Your parents know how capable you are."

She nodded and released a slow exhale. "I don't suppose there's anything to be done but wait."

He swallowed at her disappointment. He'd let

her down again. It was a talent at which he quite excelled.

He, however, had no qualms about being trapped in a snowy prison with her—was delighted, in fact. With another day or two, maybe she'd reveal more about this mystery fiancé of hers. With all they'd once shared with one another, it irked him that she'd yet to confess her betrothal. But confession or not, with a few more days in her company (and as her *husband*, no less), perhaps he could remind her how well they fit together. Persuade her to abandon this ridiculous notion of marrying another man.

She might not appreciate their current circumstances, but he would make the most of them.

Mr. Marley, having experienced a winter's storm or two in his years, had had the foresight to retrieve shovels from his barn the night before. He emerged from the kitchen with a pair, and Andrew turned from Aster to assist him.

She tugged on his sleeve, pulling him back to face her. He looked up, nearly drowning in her eyes as she whispered, "I—I'm glad you were the one with me last night."

His brows dipped. "Even though I drove us into a hole?"

She nodded.

"Even though I broke the wheel?"

She nodded again, her lips tilting into a half-smile.

"Even though I broke your arithmo-thingum?"

She sniffed. "You're testing the limits of my gratitude."

—

ASTER HELPED MRS. MARLEY IN the kitchen while the older girls kept watch over the younger children. She stirred a large pot of porridge as her hostess fried sausages and Betsy took down cups for tea. Every now and then, one of the children would return to deliver an eager report on how far Andrew and Mr. Marley had shoveled.

"They're nearly to the hawthorn now, Mama," Elsie said.

Betsy leaned against the kitchen worktable with a sigh. "You're so fortunate, Mrs. Grey," she said. "Your captain is ever so handsome."

This last was said breathlessly, and Aster looked at the girl from the corner of her eye. A denial was on the tip of her tongue—he was hardly *her* captain—but instead she winked at Betsy. "He is that."

"Mama says a pretty face won't guarantee beef on the table," Kitty reminded them.

"'A strong back and strong character will better

serve'," Elsie recited as she returned from her station at the parlor window. Then, "They're clearing a path to the kitchen now, Mama."

"Yes, but a pretty face doesn't hurt anyone," Betsy grumbled.

"I have a pretty face," four-year-old Daniel sang as his brother chased him round the table. "Pretty face, pretty face!"

"Children!" Mrs. Marley said in exasperation as she herded her flock from the kitchen. When she returned, she shook her head at Aster and asked, "Have you and your captain been blessed with children yet, or is this to be your first?"

Aster's cheeks warmed. Perhaps she stood too close to the fire. She shuffled a step back but continued stirring. "Um, no," she said. "We have not."

The gentlemen entered then from their new kitchen path and paused to stomp snow from their boots on a thick rug. The icy air was a relief to Aster's too-warm cheeks.

"Have not what?" Andrew, of the unnaturally large ears, asked.

She frowned repressively at him, but when he lifted his brows in innocent expectation, she relented and said, "I was just explaining to Mrs. Marley that we have not yet been blessed with children. Until now, that is." She waved a hand vaguely over her flat middle as the tips of her ears caught flame.

His eyes widened at her words before he nodded sagely. "Yes, it's true." Then he nudged Mr. Marley's elbow and added, "Although it hasn't been for a lack of diligence."

The Marleys chuckled, and Mrs. Marley colored a bit above her white lace collar. Aster gasped once Andrew's meaning became clear.

She would murder him, she thought. She'd wait until he was asleep and then ... Surely, no court would convict her if she choked him with his own muffler.

—

THE MARLEYS SEEMED CONTENT TO have two more at their breakfast table, for which Andrew was grateful. Their travel circumstances couldn't be helped, but the Marleys' hospitality certainly made them more bearable.

Breakfast was a noisy, messy affair. The younger children missed their mouths with the porridge more often than they achieved their target, and Mrs. Marley and the older girls were constantly wiping up spills. Andrew watched Aster as she cut a sausage for the youngest boy—Daniel, he thought his name was. The scene was one of pleasant, domestic disorder and he wanted it for himself. Yearned for it.

Looking up, he found her watching him. He fixed a smile on his face before shoveling in another bite of sausage.

"Can we collect boughs for the mantel? Please, Mama?" Kitty asked.

"Berries, too!"

"And mistletoe!" Betsy said.

What was this? Mistletoe? Brilliant. Bless Miss Betsy Marley.

"I'll help," Andrew offered. "And I'm sure Mrs. Grey will wish to accompany us. She has a good eye for that sort of thing."

Aster's brows rose on that assertion before Betsy clasped her arm with enthusiasm.

"Oh, yes, you must come, Mrs. Grey, and help us find the best greenery!"

Aster set her tea down before it spilled and smiled at the girl. "Of course."

CHAPTER NINE

AND SO IT WAS THAT Aster found herself bundled to the eyes, much as Andrew had been when he'd assisted Mr. Marley. Andrew tugged her closer by the strings of her cloak and lifted the muffler higher on her face.

She reached for her bonnet, but before she could settle it in place, he leaned over and kissed her forehead. Her forehead! Like she was a child, not his supposed wife, carrying his supposed babe. Although, he probably assumed he'd receive a drubbing for anything more impertinent than a forehead buss. And he would. Receive a drubbing, that was. Probably. Possibly.

She stifled a growl and followed him and the children outside.

The air was crisp, with a bite that set her eyes to watering and her nose to dripping. Woolly silence—

the sort that only a heavy snow could produce—blanketed the farm. Their tracks from the night before were long gone, erased by the blowing snow. Her toes quickly numbed in her boots, despite her thick woolen stockings.

Andrew pulled a small sled behind him and led them past the hawthorn in front of the Marley cottage—the mistletoe there was deemed too young—and past the poplar at the edge of the lane—too thin. Presently they entered a small wood next to the Marley farm, where mistletoe and holly and fir abounded.

As the children pointed out their favorite branches, Andrew lifted a saw to liberate their finds. He made a great fuss over their selections, with the overdone dramatics one acquainted with him might expect.

"This one?" he asked, holding the blade to a tiny twig on a lovely fir.

"No!" the children chorused.

"This one then? That's a fine specimen," he said and they groaned. This selection was even poorer than the first. He made a great show of cutting the tender shoot with his saw and handed it with two fingers to Daniel, who howled with laughter.

Eventually, the children convinced him to cut the proper branches, and Betsy carefully arranged them to be towed back to the cottage. Soon the sled was overflowing with greenery.

"Don't forget the mistletoe!" Betsy said.

"Right," Andrew agreed. "We're looking for goodly sized clumps, with lots of plump berries. We don't want a shortage of kisses."

Betsy giggled, then Andrew directed the children. "Miss Betsy, why don't you lead the children's search over there, and Mrs. Grey and I will search this side of the wood. Let's meet back here to see who has found the most perfect clump."

"Come, Betsy!" Daniel begged and the children went off. Aster folded her hands at her waist as Andrew turned back to her.

"What?" he said.

"Very neatly done."

"I don't know to what you refer, madam."

She just smiled. He adjusted the wool scarf higher on his face, and his words were muffled. "They're a bit energetic, aren't they?"

"You should have considered that before volunteering for this mission, Captain."

"Right. Well, we don't have long. They'll be back any moment." He took her hand and gave a tug, but she dug in her heels.

"Where are we going?" she asked.

"Were you not listening, Mrs. Grey? We're to search this side of the wood, and I aim to find the biggest clump of mistletoe anyone on this frozen lump of an island has ever seen." He dropped her hand and marched forward, his boots sinking in the soft snow.

"Biggest is not always best," she argued.

He looked back at her with a disbelieving lift of one dark brow. How did he do it, the single-eyebrow thing? He'd always had tremendous mastery over his brows while she, despite his tutelage, had never managed to achieve more than a frightened-rabbit expression.

At her silence, he turned and continued on, and she took advantage of his inattention. Taking up a handful of snow from the crook of a nearby tree, she patted it into a perfect ball. "Biggest is not always best," she repeated, "except in war."

Her aim was perfect, and her fire landed squarely on the back of his head, knocking his hat to the ground. He turned, stunned, then gave chase, lobbing hastily crafted balls of wet snow that hit their mark less often than he must have wished. She laughed and ran as fast as her stays and petticoats would allow. Which was to say, not very fast at all.

Breathing heavily, she slowed and finally stopped, turning in time to receive the full force of him as he ran toward her, a large snowball clutched in one hand.

"Oomphf," she said inelegantly as he landed atop her in the powdery snow. He rolled slightly so she didn't receive his full weight, but he was still quite . . . large. Quite . . . heavy. All male. Her breath stopped, but she didn't think it was due to her stays. His eyes narrowed, shifting from new moss to green fire that set her aflame. His scarf had come loose, and she could see the faint shadow of dark whiskers on his cheeks and above his lip. Grinning, he pulled her muffler below her chin.

"I'd recommend against firing the first shot if you don't have the artillery to back it up," he said.

"Spoken like a seasoned captain of the Queen's Army."

His eyes darkened. "I learned a thing or two in my years away. I'm not the same ne'er-do-well you knew before."

Truer words were never spoken.

Aster licked her lips and urged her heart to ease its frantic thumping. Her brain, though, had no governance over her poor heart it would seem. Her eyes darted to the tree above them, to the thick clump of mistletoe nestled in the V of two large branches and hanging directly—quite auspiciously— above them.

Andrew twisted and followed her gaze then turned back to face her. His lips curved in a slow smile as their breath puffed between them in a fine cloud. While he claimed to have changed during his time away, his smile had not. It was quintessential

Andrew—all devil and no mercy. He was going to kiss her. Her toes curled in her leather boots, and the cold (and all thoughts of his probable-possible drubbing) were forgotten as he lowered his head.

His kiss, when it finally came, was much more than the tentative pecks they'd exchanged in their youth. This kiss was bigger, brighter, faster, stronger than she'd ever imagined a kiss could be. It tipped her stomach on edge and fuzzed the edges of her mind until she ran out of superlatives.

His mouth was earnest and insistent as his large hands cradled her head in the snow. He tasted and nipped at her before pressing his lips more firmly against hers. She gripped his coat to pull him closer, warmth rising to curl around them.

This—*this!*—was what she'd been waiting for. Not just for the time that Andrew had been away, but for the whole of her life. She'd been foolish to think she could ever replace him in her heart with another.

Just when she thought they must have melted the snow beneath them, he stopped and pulled back. She stared at him in confusion, her lips cooling where his had been. She reluctantly allowed her hands to fall from his coat as disappointment flooded her.

His eyes were shadowed now like stormy seas, the sort that presaged jagged, hair-raising bolts of lightning and whipping winds. He pressed his lips in—irritation?—as he watched her. *He* was irritated with *her*?

His chest rose and fell against her until finally he rolled to one side. She lay in place, trapped by her rigid stays like a turtle encumbered by its own shell. He stood and, reaching a hand down, assisted her to her feet. He opened his mouth then closed it at her stern look.

"Don't you dare apologize, Andrew Grey." Tears threatened as she thought, dazedly, that perhaps she should apologize to him. She'd been the one to tug him closer as they'd lain in the snow. And then he'd pulled away. He couldn't have made his feelings any clearer.

She brushed snow from her skirts and righted the woolen muffler about her neck before turning to rejoin the children.

—

ANDREW FOUGHT THE URGE TO scream his frustration and retrieved his hat from the snowbank. His lips burned as if Aster had taken a gas flame to his face. He wondered if perhaps he'd suffered permanent damage.

But that kiss . . . He inhaled and slowly released the breath. They'd exchanged a few sweet and tender kisses in their youth, but that kiss . . . If he'd kissed her like that before he'd left for India, he'd never have gone. All of her had met all of him in that kiss.

But if he'd never gone to India, would he still have been Andrew Grey, ne'er-do-well and scapegrace extraordinaire? Or would he have got out of his own way long enough to make something of himself?

Not that India had forged a gentleman from him, he thought with a snort. She'd silenced what she thought to be an apology on his lips, when regret for the most sublime kiss of his life had never even occurred to him.

Instead, he'd opened his mouth to challenge her about this supposed fiancé. Because if she was so in love with the bloke, enough to spend the *rest of her days* with the man, then why had she looked at Andrew like he held the only key to the kingdom? He hadn't imagined the all-consuming fire in her eyes.

Lord, if she'd ever flashed that for anyone but him, he'd eat his hat.

But why, then, was she intent on marrying another? If it hadn't been for her sister's letter, he'd never have known. He'd still be in his Indian bungalow, counting his rupees and wondering if he'd finally made enough of himself to return while she made plans to move on from him.

What had he been thinking to stay away for so long? He should have known (and truthfully, a part of him had known) she'd not be his forever. The acknowledgment caused a burning, pinching sensation in his chest that the pressure of his fist couldn't relieve. It was almost as if he'd—No. He'd not think it. But as with any thought, once he'd determined not to think it, he couldn't help but do so.

It was almost as if he'd purposely stayed away and waited for her to move on.

But to do such a beef-witted thing was, well, beef-witted. It was the act of a coward. He'd never suffered for a lack of courage, except where she was concerned. He had bloody *medals* attesting to his bravery, for heaven's sake. He kicked at a drift of snow then winced to find a rock beneath it.

"We found the best clump, Captain Grey," Betsy proclaimed when he'd rejoined the children. "Mrs. Grey says it's the best, biggest, most perfect clump in all the county."

No, Andrew wanted to say. For he and Mrs. Grey had already found—and tested—the best, biggest, most perfect clump. But all traces of their kiss were removed from Aster's face as she waited with the children, one hand on Daniel's shoulder.

"Then by all means, this is the one we shall

have." He smiled around the ache in his chest and hefted the saw. Then he went to retrieve this mythical mistletoe.

CHAPTER TEN

THE ACHE IN ANDREW'S CHEST grew over the course of the afternoon. Aster assisted Mrs. Marley with the children, and together they strung garlands of berries and dried fruit as Mr. Marley and Andrew hung boughs at their direction.

"Not there," Aster said as Andrew balanced on a ladder. "A little higher. What do you think, girls?"

The Marley girls nodded their assent, and Andrew stretched to fix a lengthy bough of fir to the parlor's rafter.

Her smiles were ready and frequent for the Marleys, he noticed, but not once did she look at him as if she'd like an encore of their kiss. She looked, in fact, like she'd all but forgotten the incident. He pressed his irritation back where it belonged, beneath a heaping pile of self-pity.

Marley pressed a mug of ale into his hands as they watched the ladies discuss the proper placement of the kissing bough.

"Ladies and their traditions," he muttered at Andrew's elbow. "You'll have your hands full with all this nonsense once your little one comes along."

Aster, who'd never been hard of hearing, colored at that, although she didn't deign to favor them with a glance. Andrew merely nodded his agreement and stared into his ale.

"Did you have a look yet at the extra wheels in my barn?" Marley asked.

Aster did look up at that. Her eyes brightened as Marley continued.

"As I said last night, there's sure to be one that will be a fit for your carriage. And if not, there's a wheelwright not far from here who can fix you right up."

"Er, no, I haven't looked yet," Andrew replied. He avoided Aster's gaze.

Aster dropped the thread she was weaving through a pile of berries and leaned forward. "That would be wonderful, Mr. Marley, if you have a wheel that will fit. Andrew, dear, go have a look. We might be able to continue on our way sooner than we expected." She smiled sweetly as she shooed him from the room with berry-stained hands, clearly eager for them to leave.

He nodded and set his ale aside. "Yes, thank you, Marley. I'll have a look and see what's to hand."

——

THAT NIGHT, AFTER BELLIES WERE full and the Marley house had settled, Andrew and Aster assumed their respective positions in their shared room. Aster lay atop the quilt, arms crossed over her stomach as Andrew shifted on his rug. She'd left her boots on this time, and they hung off the end of the bed.

He'd quirked an eyebrow at that but had remained blessedly silent.

"It's unfortunate Mr. Marley didn't have a wheel to fit our coach," she said, picking at a thread on her dress.

"Yes," he agreed. "It's unfortunate, indeed."

"And that the wheelwright was unavailable."

He murmured another agreement. "I'll check the condition of the roads tomorrow. Perhaps try the wheelwright again."

She nodded, although he couldn't see her from his position on the rug. He lay silent on the floor below her, and she wondered if he'd fallen asleep.

Although she was anxious to reach her family and ease their worry, a large part of her didn't mind the extra time spent with Andrew. Despite his apparent disinterest in a more intimate acquaintance, she did count him as a friend. She'd missed him, and once they reached Redstone Hall, he'd depart for nearby Fernwood. She imagined she'd not see much of him before he returned to India. She swallowed the lump in her throat.

The air between them had grown uncomfortable since that toe-curling kiss, and she was eager to set it right again. She opened and closed her mouth once, twice, unsure what to say.

"Don't worry over it, Aster," he growled from the floor.

She snapped her mouth shut. Then, because it wasn't her way to remain silent, she began, "But—"

"It happened," he said. "It was pleasant, but we can forget it ever occurred if that eases your conscience."

Pleasant? He thought the most transcendental moment of her life was *pleasant*? His disinterest aside, this was why they could never be more than friends. Nothing was sacred to Andrew. Nothing mattered. He claimed he was not the same ne'er-do-well he'd once been, but he continued to pass through life without a care. That he'd done so well for himself in the army was naught but happenstance.

Then she frowned.

"Why are you out of your regimentals?"

His pause was overlong. Finally, he said, "If this

is your way of asking me to remove my clothes—"

"Stop," she said. She rose on one elbow and turned toward him. "Why are you out of your regimentals, *Captain*?"

"I cashed out," he said simply. He crooked an elbow behind his head and avoided her gaze.

"What?" She stared at him. "When? Why?"

"So many questions," he sighed, not meeting her eyes. Avoidance was Andrew's way of addressing unpleasantness.

Her lips flattened into a straight line. He had that effect on her. "All right. We'll take them one by one," she said slowly, "so as not to overtax your brain. *When* did you cash out?"

"Almost two years ago."

She inhaled and prayed for calm. "And *why* did you cash out?"

"I was injured. It was foolish, truly not more than a scratch—"

"You were injured? Where?" She spun on the bed and sat up. "Why didn't you say anything?"

"Again with the questions. Where? About twenty miles north of Bombay."

"Andrew."

He fluttered a hand over his thigh. "I took a tree to the leg. Hurt like a—Well, as I said, it wasn't more than a scratch."

She gasped, both hands flying to her mouth as

she leaned forward. She recalled again his limp the night they'd arrived at the Marleys' cottage.

"The surgeon wanted to—Well, Vicky wouldn't have me any longer, so . . . I cashed out."

"Why didn't you say anything?" Her eyes burned and she longed to crush him to her, but she said only, "Do your parents know?"

He snorted. "No. They would have been on the first boat to Bombay. My mother is a fine surgeon, but her bedside manner is a bit smothering."

"Well, of course it is. She's your mother."

Aster turned and lay back on the bed again. "I've been writing to Captain Grey these past years. How have you been receiving my letters?"

"A friend—you recall me writing of Monty Doyle?—he was gracious enough to pass my post along when he was able, although I fear his service was somewhat irregular."

"Are you still a captain? How does that work?"

A pause, then, "In the strictest terms, no."

She spun and sat up again. "You're impersonating an officer of the British Army?"

"Shhh," he said. "Keep your voice down. Please. And to answer your question—which I find very offensive, by the way—no. I've not held myself out to be an officer since I left the army. The fact that *you* have insisted on calling me Captain—"

"Because I didn't know otherwise," she hissed.

"Well, now you do."

She lay back down and folded one arm over her eyes. Two *years*. He'd been free of the army and living a life in India for nearly *two years* and hadn't bothered to come home. She'd been waiting for him for . . . for nothing. A lump seized her throat, and it was some moments before she could speak again.

"How long will you remain in England before you return?"

An uncomfortable silence passed. They'd never used to have trouble with silence. He finally said, "My plans are as yet undecided."

"What"—she cleared her throat and tried again—"what have you been doing all this time?"

"Filigree."

She heard him sit up, and she lowered her arm. Surely, she'd misheard. "Filigree?"

"And gemstones. Trading mostly, but I met a jeweler—a Marathi *karagira*—who showed me some of the old ways. Aster, you should see the designs—"

She stifled a sob. "Why are you here, Andrew?" she whispered. She turned her head to see him studying his hands.

Finally, he said, "I think that should be rather obvious."

"I know we're trapped by the snow, but why are you here now, with me? Why did you buy my coach—"

"And the pair."

"—And the pair. Why did you tell the Marleys we're husband and wife, with . . . with—"

"With a babe on the way?"

"Yes," she hissed.

He turned and lay back on the rug, crossing his hands behind his head.

"What do you want me to say, Aster?"

A long moment passed. She didn't answer, and he didn't press. She thought he'd fallen asleep, then he asked, "Have you seen my parents recently? Are they as well as their letters have led me to believe?"

And just like that, he erased the past minutes as if they'd never occurred. She sighed. "They're well, although your brother was recently sent down from Harrow."

"Again? Lord, what a scapegrace."

CHAPTER ELEVEN

Andrew rose before Aster—again. She'd never been much of one for mornings. He hadn't either, to be truthful, but the army had cured him of that. She lay curled on her side, hands tucked beneath her chin, amber sparking from the braid that was unraveling about her cheek. Her boots hung off the end of the bed. Boots!

That she'd worn her shoes to bed surely spoke of her discomfort with their current situation, although he couldn't, in truth, blame her. He'd forced a marriage *and* impending motherhood on her in no short order. No lady would have taken that half as gracefully as Aster had. He just hoped her father never learned of this escapade. He'd jested with her about his impending disembowelment, but there had been a grain of truth to his words.

Harry Corbyn was a bookish man, but solidly

built, and he doted on his children. Their families had been close for years, since long before Andrew had been born, but he didn't wish to test the man's forbearance any more than necessary. Although, as he looked on his "wife" he thought it might be a bit late for prudence.

He collected his coat from a peg by the door, and Aster stirred. Mumbled something in her sleep that sounded like a curse. She must be dreaming of him. He smiled. Cursing him or kissing him, he supposed it didn't much matter as long as he was in her dreams.

"Andrew?" she said as he reached for the knob.

He paused, swallowing as she raised her head. She was delightfully mussed, the dying fire highlighting the curve of her cheek, sleep clouding her eyes, and despair washed over him. He had to have her—in his life, in his bed, in his arms—but he didn't know that he'd ever achieve such a lofty aim. He thought the race might have been lost before he'd even realized it was on.

He forced a smile to his face. "Good morning."

She pushed herself up. "You're going to check the condition of the road?"

"Yes. The sun will be up soon. I thought to go at first light."

"I'm coming with you." She swung her legs to the floor and tossed her braid behind her.

"I won't be gone long," he said and reached for the doorknob once again.

"Don't go without me," she said and, because he couldn't deny her, he agreed. "I'll wait for you downstairs."

—

ASTER HURRIED THROUGH HER ABLUTIONS, splashing icy water on her face from the basin on the vanity. She cleaned her teeth in a rush, lest Andrew leave without her. It would be just like him, if only to be contrary.

Swinging her cloak about her shoulders, she grabbed her bonnet from a peg and hurried for the stairs. She was relieved to see he waited for her at the bottom, idly tapping his hat against his thigh, and she wondered again about his wound. He had a talent for understatement—second only to his talent for making her smile—and she was fairly confident his injury had been much worse than he'd let on. Certainly, it had been serious enough to remove him from the Queen's service.

Her stomach pinched to think of him lying in a field hospital, thousands of miles from home and everyone who loved him. Thousands of miles from her. No matter that they'd been watching the same star for years, he might as well have been on the moon. He looked up and tossed his careless grin at her as she descended. Pasting a smile on her face, she swept toward the door.

She was conscious of him at her side as she carefully picked her way through the fields, through drifts considerably shrunken by the previous day's sunshine. Wood smoke from the Marley chimneys laced the air with its comforting sting, and the only sound was their feet crunching the crisp snow.

They reached the road at the end of the fields. It stretched in either direction, pristine and white, with naught more than a few intrepid horse tracks to mar its surface. It was still snow-covered, but passable.

The coach appeared much as they'd left it. Ice dripped from the roof to dot the snow below, and the shaft rested empty against the road, waiting for the horses to be hitched. All they needed was a serviceable wheel, and they could be on their way. She'd soon be reunited with her family at Redstone Hall, and Andrew could return to nearby Fernwood.

The thought should have brought more joy. She was certainly eager to see her family again, especially as her sister would leave soon for Africa. It would be a year or more before they saw one another next. But returning to Redstone Hall meant she'd be one step closer to Andrew leaving her again.

She fixed a smile on her face and turned to him.

"The road is much improved," she said.

He stood with his hands on his hips, face shadowed by the brim of his hat. "It is," he agreed.

She turned her attention to the broken wheel. "How far is the wheelwright?"

"His shop is just a short distance the other side of Marley's farm."

She nodded. "Shall we go then?"

He was silent for a moment, his brow furrowed in thought. He opened his mouth as if to say something important, and she held her breath. "Yes, let's go," he said. "You'll be at Redstone Hall with your family by nightfall," he promised.

She released her breath in disappointment.

"What?" he asked softly. "Is that not fast enough for Faster Aster?"

She directed a scowl at him. "I told you no one calls me that anymore." *Not since you left.*

He snorted, and she took a step back at the hardness in his eyes. "No one? Or perhaps this gentleman to whom you've affianced yourself has a better pet name for you? What could it be?" He tapped his chin in mocking consideration.

Her stomach dipped uncomfortably. He knew of her betrothal? Who had told him?

"Asterisk?"

Her scowl intensified.

"No? Perhaps Asteroid then? That's more fitting."

"Mr. Church wouldn't be so ridiculous," she said, advancing on him as far as her bonnet brim would allow.

"Mr. Church? That's his name? Well, you have my felicitations. He sounds quite respectable. And old." He spat the words *respectable* and *old*. Andrew could be such a . . . such a *child* at times.

"Mr. Church *is* quite respectable. He's a very upstanding gentleman, and he's not old at all. He's only five and thirty."

"Precisely. *Old*."

"Five and thirty is not old."

"We're only twenty-four."

"*You're* only twenty-four, Andrew. I'm twenty-six. Lord, but you were never good at maths." He blinked, and a devil urged her to add, "At any rate, Mr. Church will make a fine husband." Just not for her.

His voice lowered and the fight seemed to go out of him. "And here I thought that was my office."

"Yours?" she asked incredulously. "Because of this . . . this absurdity?" She waved her hand to encompass the snow and the carriage and the Marley farm.

"No, Aster. Because of the vows we spoke."

It was her turn to blink. "We were little more than children, Andrew. Surely, you don't think whispered promises and a woven bit of twisted weeds made us married?"

He stared at her for a moment more before turning on his heel with a crunch of snow. As he crossed to the fields, she thought she heard him say, "We were as good as."

"You were no husband," she called to his back as she hurried to catch up. "A husband wouldn't have left me for *years* to seek fortune and adventure."

He stopped and turned abruptly, and she nearly fell backward. She resisted the urge to kick his shin, but only just.

"And a wife would have waited," he said. "She certainly wouldn't have engaged herself *to another man*." His words emerged as a soft roar, and she was reminded of the Indian tigers he'd written about.

"Then I suppose we were both bound for disappointment."

"I suppose so."

They walked the rest of the way to the wheelwright's shop in silence.

———

MR. CHURCH. THE FIANCÉ HAD a name. Andrew's hands had grown uncomfortably damp in his gloves, and he fought a wave of nausea. He wondered if the man was a fellow mathematician.

Would he and Aster spend their evenings discussing sums and equations and . . . whatever it was that mathematicians found so intriguing?

His feet ate up the distance to the wheelwright's shop. Twice he had to stop so Aster didn't fall too far behind, which he was certain irritated her. If she could be irritated any further, that was.

He kept his silence, unsure what to say to repair the rift between them. He formed an apology in his mind, but the words sounded more bitter than sincere, even in his own head. It wasn't often that his mind issued a proper warning on the things he said *before* he said them, so when it did, he tried to listen. Accordingly, he kept his words to himself.

They were successful in finding the wheelwright, and as they left his shop, he offered the man an additional, exorbitant sum to replace the wheel for him. While he was certain he could manage the repair himself—he'd been a captain in Her Majesty's Army, for heaven's sake—he felt expediency was more important than pride or economy at this juncture. The sooner they could complete this damnable journey, the better.

Aster marched ahead of him as if the enemy was at her elbow. Soon they neared the edge of the wood near Marley's farm, her blue cloak a glorious, bright foil to the white all around. His Aster was like a wondrous star against the inky night, only in reverse. *His Aster.* How long had he thought of her thus? It would take time to break himself of the habit. Suddenly he was so very tired. All the energy of their earlier argument leached out of him and he stopped.

"Aster," he said softly.

She took two more steps then turned. He held his hand to her and after a moment's hesitation, she retraced her steps. He took her hand in his, cursing the gloves that separated their skin. Her nose was red, jaw trembling above her scarf and eyes shining with unshed tears.

"I'm sorry," he said simply, and she sniffed before giving him a watery smile.

"I'm sorry as well," she said. "I don't enjoy arguing with you."

"That's a blatant falsehood," he said gently, then, "This Mr. Church"—he inhaled—"he's a good man?"

She hesitated, as if uncertain of the wisdom of replying. Then she said slowly, "Mr. Church is a kind man."

"Does he . . . make your heart sing?"

A tear finally broke free and trailed down her cheek to disappear in the wool of her scarf. "He's a good man," she said with another sniff.

He tugged her toward him. She gazed up at him and his eyes dropped to her lips. They were soft and tempting, but he ducked his head beneath the brim of her bonnet and pressed a kiss to her cheek instead, inhaling the lemony scent of her hair. His lips lingered on the satiny smoothness of her skin before he reluctantly pulled away.

"I only want your happiness," he said.

She bit her lip and nodded. "And I, yours. Are you happy, Andrew?"

She peered at him as if trying to see into his soul, and he resisted the impulse to turn away. He forced a carefree smile to his face instead and spoke around the lump in his throat. "Always."

He kept her hand in his as they walked out of the wood. Held tightly to her as they crossed Marley's foreyard. Didn't let her go as they entered the cottage. Didn't see the horse tied in front until it was too late.

"Aster." The voice was low and familiar, but harder than he recalled.

"Papa!"

Harry Corbyn stood framed in the parlor doorway, eyeing their joined hands. Andrew let her go as Aster pulled away.

CHAPTER TWELVE

ASTER ALLOWED HERSELF TO BE folded into her father's strong, familiar embrace. She checked the sob that threatened to erupt and concentrated on the familiar scent of his cologne as his arms tightened around her.

"Captain Grey," he said above her head. She pulled away to see his jaw jump as he stared at Andrew.

"Hush, Papa," she whispered, conscious of the Marley clan standing behind him. "I shall explain later."

He looked down at her, his grey eyes, so like her own, silently communicating that he intended to have the entire story from her with no prevarication. It was a look he'd perfected over the past decades but had rarely used in recent years. At least on her. She suspected her brother Edmund still required it at times. At her nod of agreement, his eyes warmed behind his spectacles.

"We became worried when you didn't arrive," he said. "I assured your mother you would have remained in London until the weather passed, but she was equally certain you would have pressed on."

"I—we—were eager to reach Kent," Aster said. "We're grateful to the Marleys for taking us in."

"As am I," he said with a tight smile and a nod toward Mr. Marley.

"The wheelwright assured me the coach will be set to rights shortly," Andrew said. "I'll go collect our things." And with that, he turned and took the stairs two at a time. Coward.

Aster removed her bonnet and moved to follow. "I should assist Andrew," she said, but her father held her back with a hand on her shoulder.

"Your husband has things well in hand, I'm certain," he said, with added emphasis on *husband*. Lord, this explanation would not be an easy one.

She allowed him to lead her to the settee in the parlor where they sat and passed idle conversation with the Marleys while they waited for Andrew's return.

"Are you the astronomer?" Daniel asked. Aster felt an urge to kiss the boy as her father's rigid posture relaxed somewhat while he entertained the children's questions.

Andrew thumped about above their heads for a suspiciously long time before she heard him on the stairs. She suspected he was delaying the inevitable interview with her father, whereas she'd always preferred to approach unpleasant tasks directly. When he finally appeared, laden with his haversack and her valise, she jumped from the settee in relief.

The sooner they satisfied her father's questions, the better for all. She didn't *truly* believe he'd run Andrew through with his pencil.

—

ANDREW KNEW IT WAS NAUGHT but cowardice that had sent his feet flying up the stairs, and he wasn't too prideful to admit it. But he could only draw his task out for so long before he'd have to face Aster's father and his questions.

He took his time packing his comb and tooth powder into his haversack, and by force of habit confirmed the small leather pouch was still tucked where he had secured it. Although, he reasoned, if Aster was truly lost to him, its contents hardly mattered any longer.

Next, he opened her valise to deposit a handful of pins from the vanity but stopped when a tied handkerchief at the top of her bag shifted and rattled.

Her arithmo-whatever. The device he'd broken

when he'd stepped on her bag in the snow. From the sounds of it, he'd given the thing a proper coshing. It was but one more way he'd let her down.

Sighing, he tucked the handkerchief with its rattling bits into his pocket. Perhaps he could find a way to repair it (which was doubtful) or replace it. He didn't know where to go about finding such a device, but he had heaps of money now and no wife to spend it on. Surely someone, somewhere, had heard of such a thing.

He closed the valise, hefted his haversack to his shoulder and readied himself for his sentencing—rather, his *accounting*—with Harry Corbyn.

As he reached the door, he looked back one more time, a slow smile tilting his lips as he pictured Aster on the bed, fully dressed to her boots. This was one camp he'd not soon forget.

He started to pull the door closed, then his eye caught on Aster's book, tucked beneath her pillow. He crossed to the head of the bed and retrieved it, juggled the bags a bit, then hearing Corbyn's impatient voice below, stuffed the book in his coat pocket opposite her thingummy.

Finally, resigned that he couldn't delay any longer, he descended the stairs.

——

ASTER EXPRESSED HER APPRECIATION TO Mrs. Marley

and the children while her father and Andrew exchanged a few words with Mr. Marley. She couldn't tell, but she suspected one or both of them was trying to compensate the man for his family's hospitality.

As her *husband*, it was Andrew's right and obligation, and her father, realizing he couldn't argue the matter without raising unwanted questions, finally acquiesced. Mr. Marley shook Andrew's hand, then their small party took their leave of the Marleys.

Aster felt pulled in two as she watched Andrew enter the barn to retrieve the coach horses. One foot wanted to follow him while the other remained firmly next to her father as he untied his mount. She hadn't made up her mind yet when Andrew emerged. He eyed them uncertainly before leading the way across the field, reins in one hand and her valise in the other.

"Aster," her father said, and she turned to him. He'd drawn the horse to a stone mounting block in the Marley's foreyard. "Climb aboard, sweeting."

She watched in dismay as Andrew, who was now yards ahead, grew more distant. Finally, she turned back to her father. She mounted the horse, settled her skirts, and he climbed up behind her. His arms circled her as he took up the reins, and they followed Andrew to the road.

"Papa," she began.

"Not now, Aster." His voice rumbled at her back, his tension apparent, but she couldn't remain silent.

"Please don't be angry with Andrew."

"Not now."

She swallowed. She was to receive the Disappointed Silence then. It was his most powerful punishment, especially for one such as herself who preferred an immediate reckoning. She didn't think he even realized the effect his silence wielded. Although (or perhaps because) it was an infrequent tactic, it had always been enough to set her and her siblings cowering in shame. Her mother was the only one of them who could ever tease him out of it, although they'd all tried at various points.

She settled back against him with a sigh as the horse moved beneath them.

They reached the road and she saw that the wheelwright had, indeed, set the wheel right. The coach sat properly, no longer askew, atop a new wheel. Andrew hitched the horses to the shaft and turned to await them.

Her father didn't stop but kept his horse's head aimed toward their destination.

"Papa," Aster said suddenly.

He didn't reply or react.

"Papa! You must stop."

Andrew, his gaze wary, watched them pass from his place at the horses' heads. After a few more paces, her father finally stopped the horse. "What is it, Aster?"

She shifted and turned to look back at Andrew — her dear, dear friend. No matter that she'd always wanted more of him, he would always be that. She said, "Andrew promised to see me safely to Redstone Hall."

Her father's arms tightened around her, and she closed her eyes. Opened them again when her father's arms relaxed.

"What are you saying, Aster?"

She looked at Andrew, who'd straightened at the horses' heads. "I'm saying Andrew deserves the opportunity to fulfill his promise."

Andrew looked at her in confusion for a moment, then he began to smile. At her father's glare, he stopped and pressed his lips.

Her father directed his next words at Andrew. "Don't think for a moment that this is forgiven, just because you're Julian's son."

"Of course not. Sir. May I just say —"

"No, you may not."

"Papa," Aster chastised softly.

"You wish to ride with Andrew?" His voice was gruff.

"I do."

She watched her father's face, his jaw ticking in annoyance before he finally relented with a sigh, "Very well." He gave Andrew a short nod.

And Andrew, bless him, didn't hesitate. He approached her father's horse and held his arms up as she slid down. He caught her neatly and led her, very proper-like, to the door of the coach. He handed her in and settled the blanket over her knees as her father took up a position beside the coach.

And thus, they returned to Redstone Hall.

CHAPTER THIRTEEN

ANDREW'S PARENTS RESIDED IN LONDON, but his father had been raised at Fernwood Manor. The comfortable country estate was separated from Redstone Hall by a small wood and Bellamy Hill, where one could find the best view of the North Downs.

This Redstone Hall was the very same where Aster's mother, the only child and daughter of the Earl of Ashford, had been born. Accordingly, Andrew and Aster and their siblings had spent many holidays beneath the (often lax) eyes of their grandparents' servants, exploring the Hill between the two estates, dipping toes into the nearby pond when they weren't supposed to and essentially running about like savages.

This was also where Aster had been christened Faster Aster after defeating Andrew once again in a race to the top of the Hill. That he suspected her victory had come through less than honorable means, he'd kept to himself. Andrew had conceived the name, but her siblings had quickly adopted it, and he felt only a shade of remorse for his hand in it. As far as teasing went, he admitted now that it lacked a certain creativity, but his younger self had been pleased with the effort. There were only so many words that rhymed with 'Aster,' after all, and Master Aster simply wouldn't do.

The sun had emerged just long enough to vanquish the worst of the snow, and in so doing, transformed the beautiful, crystalline landscape to mud. The coach was covered in the stuff, as was Andrew. Mr. Corbyn, he was happy to see, was not immune either.

Aster's father had spoken to him once during the three-hour drive, which was both more and less than he expected. Drawing alongside Andrew, he said, "I'll extend my daughter the courtesy of speaking to her first about this matter, and then I'll expect a full accounting."

Andrew nodded once, and that, apparently, had been that. Corbyn had fallen back to Andrew's left, leaving him to drive the man's daughter in relative peace.

Snow-speckled valleys stretched before them, blending into the near-white of the winter sky. As they rounded the final curve, Redstone Hall came into view, sprawled amidst a thick cluster of poplar and sycamore. Her grandfather's domed observatory punctuated the northwest corner like a giant period while a large wooden structure marked the top of Bellamy Hill. Her father's telescope, which had drawn a number of tourists and journalists in its day. He wondered if it still did.

Aster had often laughed about the literal tendencies of her ancestors, who'd named Redstone Hall for the color of the stone forming its wings. In fact, as children, they'd held a contest to see who could devise the most creative name for the pile. To his recollection, Aster had won (of course), with something like *Le Feu Rouge*. Or The Red Fire, to those who'd not excelled at their French lessons. Which he hadn't.

The coach crunched over gravel as it entered the circular drive. He wasn't surprised to see a line of people in front of the manor's large double doors, including Aster's mother and her grandparents, sisters and brother.

Corbyn dismounted and opened the carriage door before Andrew could even step off the box. He paused in the act of tying the reins as Aster looked up at him.

"Thank you for seeing me home safely," she said.

"Always," he whispered, then cleared his throat

as Corbyn looked on.

"Give our best to your family," Corbyn said in dismissal, and Andrew nodded. Flicking the reins once more, he drove on.

—

"Papa," Aster said in whispered censure. "You didn't have to be so rude. Should we not have invited Andrew in for tea before sending him on his way?"

"No."

"Aster," her mother said, drawing her attention. "We were so worried, but I see it was for naught." Her mother enfolded her in a warm hug—not the tepid sort usually reserved for the granddaughters of earls, but a genuine, rib-crushing embrace.

"Mama," Aster laughed when she could breathe again, then she greeted her grandparents and siblings. Her mother quickly recognized the tension in her father's frame and studied them in confusion, her face clearing only when her grandmother spoke.

"Dearest, your coachman was the very image of young Andrew Grey," Lady Ashford said from behind Lord Ashford's wheeled chair. "Did you not think the resemblance uncanny?"

Her father was out of hearing as he led his horse to the stables, so Aster said, "It *was* Andrew, *Grand-*

mère. He is just now returned from India to visit his family."

"That was Andrew?" Helen asked. Aster looked at her sister sharply as Helen's surprise had seemed a bit exaggerated. "Why, he's so much darker and larger than I remember. So much more handsome."

"He's just as handsome as he always was," Aster said. "You only think that because you were a child when last you saw him."

"I was not. I was seventeen, the same age as Andrew."

"Precisely. A child."

"Hmm. And how did you come to be riding in a coach driven by our old friend?" Helen asked.

Aster opened and closed her mouth, uncertain how to respond. Finally, she opted for a vague version of the truth.

"My coachman received a better offer at the last minute, and Andrew was already traveling this way. It was the most expedient choice."

There. Let her sister make of that what she wished.

Helen harrumphed and strode ahead, her marching feet crunching the gravel as Aster reflected on her own words to her sister.

A child. At seventeen, Andrew had not been much more than a child when he'd joined Her Majesty's army and sailed out of Aster's life. She'd not stopped to think before how brave he'd been. Or how terrified he must have felt. She'd been too caught up in her own misery to think of his. An uncomfortable lump formed in her throat, and she swallowed as her father caught up with her.

"Aster. Join me in the observatory, please."

It wasn't a request. Her reckoning had arrived. Finally. She smiled and nodded, even as the rest of her family looked on in curiosity. She passed two ruby-coated footmen and entered the manor to the familiar scents of aged oak, lemon and beeswax.

Her grandfather's observatory was accessible through a narrow transit room that angled off one corner of the main house. A large Greek-style arch framed the entrance, and inside the rounded room, more Greek columns supported the second-story domed ceiling. Clerestory windows ringed the space to bounce the day's weak sunshine off the white walls. A pier, centered in the room, held a massive telescope, and two counterweights hung off a small shutter in the dome. Her father leaned against the wall opposite the telescope, arms crossed in his Silent Disappointment stance.

Now that the time was at hand, she found herself uncharacteristically reluctant to face her father's questions. She tugged on the shorter weight and watched as the shutter opened with a groan to reveal the colorless winter sky.

"Aster," her father growled.

"What do you wish to know?"

He uncrossed his arms to rub the back of his neck. "How is it that I found my daughter seeking shelter with the Marleys as Captain Grey's *wife*? The last I heard, you were engaged to Mr. Church. Your mother hasn't stopped talking about the wedding preparations for the last month."

She released a sigh. He hadn't heard the bit about her "interesting condition" then, for she was certain he would have led with that. She opted to address the easiest part of his question first.

"Papa, Mr. Church and I have determined we don't suit," she said softly.

Her father straightened and came off the wall. "When did this happen? Before or after you encountered Captain Grey?"

"Before. Mr. Church is a good man, a fine gentleman, but he—" Her voice caught and she swallowed. "He doesn't make my heart sing," she finished.

"Aster." Her father folded her in his arms for the second time that day and pressed his chin atop her head. She sniffed into his navy cravat and the tears came. Great, soggy, nose-dripping tears.

His hands soothed her back as she hiccoughed into his chest. "Shall I bring your mother?" he asked.

She pressed her hands to his chest. "N—no," she

stuttered. "I'm sorry, Papa. I'm too old to be watering your shirtfront."

"You're never too old. That's what it's there for," he said gruffly. "Now, you've answered my question about Mr. Church, and I'm sorry for it, but kindly explain how I came to find you with Captain Grey. Have you married *him*? If he's persuaded you into some havey-cavey business—"

"No," she laughed. "I've not married Andrew." And then she explained about the snowstorm and the hole and the broken wheel. "Andrew was doing what he thought was best to protect my reputation when he introduced us as Mr. and Mrs. Grey. I don't think any harm was truly done."

She opted to exclude the details regarding their shared sleeping arrangements, although her father was not a fool. He'd probably drawn his own conclusions.

"But I don't understand how Andrew came to be driving your coach in the first place."

She bit her lip. "He purchased it," she said softly.

Her father frowned and shook his head. "I'm sorry, I thought you said he purchased your coach."

"And the pair."

His eyebrows dipped in a steep V. "Why, that's the most bacon-brained—Oh, I see. It's Andrew."

"Yes," she said, lips curving into a wobbly smile. "It's Andrew. You know he can be a bit impulsive."

"He comes by it honestly, I suppose. His father has always been a scapegrace." Then he straightened and resumed his serious face. "But by all rights, he should be standing up with you, after the risk he put to your reputation."

"No, Papa," Aster said hurriedly. "Please don't force the matter."

"But—"

"Papa, I beg you will not insist on anything so archaic. I've no wish to marry Andrew like this."

"Like this?"

"I've no wish to marry Andrew," she amended.

He closed his eyes and pinched the bridge of his nose. "Just once," he said, "I wish these matters would fall to your mother to address."

"Oh, they have, I assure you," Aster said, thinking of her siblings. The alarm on her father's face would have been comical if her heart hadn't been so numb. He looked up to the open dome, hands on his hips, and sighed. She was reminded of the nights—more than she could count—when she and her siblings had watched the stars with him. He'd pointed out the constellations and helped them track the planets through the seasons.

"Papa," she said, "do you recall the game we used to play—seven stars for seven nights?"

He turned back to face her, a smile on his face. "I do. Count seven stars for seven nights—"

"—and the first person you see on the eighth day will be your true love," she finished.

He watched her for a beat before comprehension dawned. "You counted the stars, and the first person you saw was Andrew. Sweeting, that doesn't signify. It's just a—"

"No," she said, shaking her head. "It wasn't Andrew."

His brows lifted. "No? Then who?"

"Do you remember Jenkins, Grandfather's last butler?"

He snorted. "Poor, old Jenkins? He passed, what, nearly fifteen years ago."

"And then it was you, a couple of times." He smiled at that, but she continued. "Then Grandfather's gardener. The butcher's delivery boy. You see the pattern. But each time, I *wanted* it to be Andrew."

Her father moved to stand before her. He placed his hands on her shoulders and said, "Have you told him as much?"

She swallowed. "He left, Papa. He left for nearly *seven years*."

"Why has he come back?"

"He was injured. He cashed out of the army." *Nearly two years ago.* She frowned in confusion. Why had he returned *now*? At her confused silence, her father lowered his hands and continued.

"When you set out to prove one of your differential geometry theorems, you attack it with a single-minded intensity that I think must have come from your mother."

She lifted her brows at him in disbelief. "Says the pot."

"My point," he said, "is that you begin with the known facts. And then . . ."

"And then . . . I follow a series of logical deductions to arrive at the conclusion."

"Precisely. Don't retreat from the conclusion."

CHAPTER FOURTEEN

AFTER ANDREW SURPRISED HIS GRANDMOTHER'S stable master with two new mounts of dubious origin and a traveling coach of even less distinction, he approached the steps to Fernwood. The butler opened the door before he could knock.

"Master Andrew," he said, a smile teasing the corner of his lips. "Or rather, Captain Grey. Welcome back to Fernwood." The retainer stood at attention, heels together, bald head gleaming beneath thin filaments of silver hair.

"Master Andrew is fine, Crutchfield. Captain Grey makes me feel as old as my father."

"Just so," Crutchfield said, taking his hat and closing the door behind Andrew.

"Who's old?" His father's voice preceded him as Dr. Julian Grey emerged from the library adjacent to the entry. At just a shade over fifty, his father had managed to maintain his lean form. His hair, Andrew was interested to see, had begun a marginal tactical retreat from his forehead, but it was still dark, with only a trace of silver at the temples.

"Father," Andrew said, and a wave of homesickness nearly undid him as his father folded him in a manly embrace. He closed his eyes as the familiar, spicy scent of his father's cologne brought the sting of memories crashing over him.

"Charlie," his father called, but his mother already stood in the doorway of the library. She held one hand to her throat as she gazed at Andrew, and her eyes were suspiciously moist, her mouth wobbling as she tried to smile.

Andrew looked at her in surprise—his mother was not normally prone to overly feminine bouts of emotion. "What's this, Mother? Tears?"

She gave him a watery laugh and looped her arms around him as she kissed his cheek. "You're home," she whispered. His pocket rattled at her squeezing, and he was reminded of Aster's arithmo-bits. And her book.

His mother stepped out of the circle of his arms, a question in her gaze as she eyed his pocket.

"It's nothing," he told her, wishing it were true.

"We weren't sure when your business in London would be concluded," she said, smoothing her hands along his coat front before stepping away.

"Your trunks arrived two days ago, and Crutchfield had them placed in your old room. I'm sure you'll wish to change and refresh yourself from your travels."

Before he could excuse himself to do just that, another voice hailed him from the foot of the stairs. "Andrew!"

He turned to see a young man with his mother's blue eyes and the same dark hair Andrew shared with his father.

"John? Look how you've grown!"

His mother herded them into the library as John chuckled. "I should hope so."

When he'd last seen his youngest brother, John had been a gangly lad of ten. Now, he must be a gangly lad approaching seventeen. The same age Andrew had been when he'd sailed for India.

"I heard you've been sent down again."

John's eyes widened. "The news has sailed all the way to India then?"

Andrew snorted. "Your antics are hardly that legendary. I heard from . . . a friend on the road from London." He ignored his mother's curious look.

John eyed their parents warily and rubbed the back of his neck. "Longshanks caught me in the pub—"

"Again?" Andrew asked. While his brother's compatriots had the good sense to hide themselves when a proctor entered the local tavern, John hadn't yet mastered the art, it would seem.

"Again," their parents agreed in tight unison.

"My mates and I, we were having such a grand time of it, and I just didn't realize ol' Longshanks had made an appearance. I tell you, he creeps about like a phantom," John said to Andrew. Then he added to their mother, "I promise not to get caught again."

"Or," Andrew said, squeezing John's shoulder, "you could avoid the pub altogether, at least until your term has ended." Lord, had that bit of prudery come from him? He sounded like . . . an *adult*. When had that happened?

John laughed as if Andrew had made a joke, then quickly sobered at his brother's frowning expression.

"As if getting caught in the pub isn't bad enough," their mother said repressively, "you were supposed to be studying for your maths exam. You'll never complete sixth form at this rate."

"I've half a mind to let Aster Corbyn have her way with you," their father said, crossing his arms.

What? Andrew cleared his throat. "What do you mean?" he asked.

"Miss Aster Corbyn—Harry Corbyn's bluestocking daughter," John explained. "She tutored me last year. She's positively terrifying when it comes to algebra proofs." He shivered slightly, but the gleam in his eye said he wouldn't mind overmuch if Miss Corbyn had her way with him.

"I know who Aster Corbyn is," Andrew grumbled, to which John's only reply was a raised brow.

Andrew made his excuses after a bit and retired to his room. Crutchfield sent a man to clean his boots and brush the mud from his coat. Before he turned the garment over to him, he gingerly removed Aster's knotted handkerchief and book, setting them on his bedside table.

Once he was alone again, he lifted her book, smiling to see the title embossed on the burgundy leather spine. *On the Influence of Signs in Mathematical Reasoning.* Trust Aster to find enjoyment in such dull reading. He riffled the pages idly and something fluttered to the carpet at his feet.

A pressed flower? He bent to retrieve it and saw that it wasn't a pressed flower, but a *woven bit of twisted weeds*, carefully preserved between the pages of her book. His stomach dipped, sending warmth clear to his fingertips as he turned the fragile ring before the window's feeble light.

Surely, you don't think a woven bit of twisted weeds made us married.

He recalled well the day he'd given her the ring. It had been the same day he'd informed her he'd signed on with the army.

The same day they'd sat at the base of her father's telescope atop Bellamy Hill and whispered provisional vows to one another.

The same day they'd promised to watch the stars together from across the seas, when he'd promised to return to her, and she'd promised to wait for him. She'd always been impatient. He closed his eyes until the stinging passed.

Next, he lifted her handkerchief, wincing to feel the pieces rattle about inside. He slowly untied the ends and unwrapped the pile, frowning as he tried to make sense of the myriad bits of gold and glass. He'd never seen one of these devices, but it looked an awful lot like a . . . like a common pocket watch. It *was* a common pocket watch.

Perhaps a gift for Aster's betrothed, Mr. Church? Irritated at yet another reminder of her defection, he frowned and began to set the pieces aside. He felt no urging to repair her gift for another man. Then the outside of the case caught his attention. Or rather, the engraving there. He moved closer to the window for a better look. It was a pair of initials: AC.

C for Church?

Then he peered more closely and saw that it wasn't a C, but a G. AG. His heart ticked a notch faster, realizing the significance before his head did.

He turned the piece over to see more inscribed on what would have been the inside of the watch's case. *For a man of some consequence.*

AG. Andrew Grey. She'd bought him a watch.

She'd kept his ring.

A knock sounded on the mahogany door. "Enter," he called, his mind far from Fernwood.

His mother's head appeared around the edge of the wood. She saw the expression on his face and hurried to him.

"Andrew?" she asked softly. "What is it? I knew when you arrived that something wasn't right."

He forced his eyes to focus on her face. Some of her beloved red curls had escaped her pins to frame her temples.

"Were you injured?" she asked. "Is that why you're not wearing your regimentals?"

He was tempted to lie so she wouldn't worry, but she'd always been able to ferret out his untruths. "Yes, Mother," he admitted, "but it was a long time ago. I'm hearty and whole now, so you needn't worry."

Her eyes raked his form as if she tried to see beneath his wool to the injury beneath. She was a surgeon through and through.

"Mother," he said, placing a hand on her shoulder. "I'm well."

"Then what troubles you?" She sat on the edge

of the bed and arranged her skirts.

He looked at her then down at the mangled watch case in his hand. Something on his face must have given his thoughts away.

"You're thinking of Aster." Her words were a statement rather than a question, but he nodded. And suddenly, as if he was a repentant boy of five who'd just broken her favorite vase, his confession came flooding out. He told her how he'd purchased Aster's coach and pair. How they'd become stranded in the snow and their time at the Marleys.

"Mr. and Mrs. Grey," she said with a smile. "It sounds lovely, if a little reckless. Your father and I always assumed you and Aster would—well. What will you do now?"

What would he do? He'd spent the past years acquiring a fortune. Making something of himself so he could make Aster his. As was typical, he'd been too slow. Too late. He was at a loss what to do next. Return to India? Set himself up in London? None of his options held any appeal without Aster by his side.

"What do you think I should do?"

"I can't tell you that, Andrew," she said, as he'd known she would. She hesitated then added, "But I can tell you that love—true love—takes courage. Courage to trust another person's love and courage to give your heart into their keeping. You can't love and hold onto your heart at the same time."

He nodded, her words washing over him. He reached for them, tried to wrap them about his own experience. And then, like a wooden kaleidoscope he'd had as a child, bits and pieces turned and shifted to form something wonderful. A brilliant truth he'd been a fool to miss.

The pocket watch engraved with his initials.

The woven bit of twisted weeds that Aster must have moved from book to book for nearly seven years.

And the final piece that clicked into place: when he'd asked if her Mr. Church made her heart sing, she'd sniffed and said only, *He's a good man.*

Aster wouldn't marry her Mr. Church. She *couldn't* marry him when she loved Andrew. Lord, why was he so blasted *slow*?

"Mother," he said suddenly, and she jumped. "I must go." He kissed her cheek and added, "Don't wait supper for me."

She looked like she might protest, then she smiled and nodded and helped him into his coat.

He made it as far as his bedchamber door before he stopped, turned, and retraced his steps. Then, gathering up Aster's book (with its weeds replaced), her handkerchief (with its watch bits), and the leather pouch from his haversack, he left.

CHAPTER FIFTEEN

ANDREW WAS SHOWN INTO THE laboratory at Redstone Hall with all the pomp of a drawing room appearance at court. The footman retreated silently, drawing the doors closed behind him, and Andrew waited for Aster's father to acknowledge him.

He'd been in this room before as a boy. It was evenly divided down the middle as if by political treaty. One side—the domain of Aster's grandfather—lay in haphazard disarray with piles of papers and books teetering at table's edge. The other—her father's half—was a study in precise, regimented order with everything positioned at crisp right angles.

While Andrew belonged more in the haphazard camp, his days in the army had taught him a soldier's appreciation for order. It was difficult to muster one's troops into battle when one couldn't find the map.

He cleared his throat once, to no effect, so he clasped his hands behind his back and waited. Waiting was also a skill well-learned and oft-practiced in the army.

Finally, Corbyn looked up and then, sighing, consulted his watch. "Two hours, Captain Grey," he said. "You've only been out of my daughter's company for two hours."

"And that's two hours too long," he said. Corbyn frowned, so he added, "Sir."

Corbyn set his pencil aside and leaned back. He folded his arms across his chest in a maneuver Andrew suspected was calculated to put him on edge. He conceded it was well conceived, and he resisted the urge to shift his feet.

"My daughter has told me her version of events, Captain Grey. Pray, explain yourself."

And so he did.

"Aster and I had no choice but to seek shelter. Indeed, we were fortunate that the Marley farm was so close at hand, and I felt that presenting ourselves as a married couple would present the least danger to your daughter's reputation."

So far, Corbyn seemed appeased. "Continue," he said.

"The bit about Aster's interesting condition . . .

that was an embellishment on my part, admittedly, but—" He stopped and swallowed when Corbyn unfolded his arms and leaned forward.

"Pardon?"

Andrew quickly aborted that line of narrative. "I know my actions were ill-advised, sir, and I want to make things right."

"Speak plainly, Captain. You refer to marriage?"

"I do."

"And if my daughter doesn't wish to marry you?"

Andrew inhaled and held the breath. He'd have to find a way to make Aster see they were meant to be together. They'd always been meant for one another.

"Let me ask you instead, Captain, *why* do you wish to marry my daughter?"

Andrew smiled. This question was an easy one. "I love her, sir. I've always loved her, and I have reason to believe she loves me as well."

Corbyn studied him for an uncomfortably long minute. Finally, he spoke. "Do you have the means to support her? She's granddaughter to an earl, but her strong lineage is nothing to the strength of her mind. She'll make her mark on the world of mathematics, and I'll not have her following the drum, living in a soldier's camp."

And so, Andrew explained his departure from the army and the nature of his finances. Corbyn listened and asked a few more questions then rubbed a hand over his jaw when Andrew finished.

"I was in your shoes once, much as I hate to admit it. I love Aster's mother more than my own life. The difference between us, Grey, is I had the sense to tell her that *before* I left for another continent."

Andrew cleared his throat uncomfortably.

"If you love her as you say," Corbyn continued, "tell her. I won't promise she'll have you, but tell her."

Dismissed, Andrew turned to go. Then he stopped. "Do—do you know where I might find her?" he asked.

"Figure it out, Grey."

Andrew nodded and left to do just that.

———

ASTER, HAVING ASCERTAINED FROM FERNWOOD'S butler that Andrew was "not at home at present," left a note for him and returned to Redstone Hall by way of Bellamy Hill. She smiled to see her father's telescope proudly pointing toward the evening sky, waiting patiently for the stars to emerge, even as she waited *impatiently* for Andrew's return.

She and her siblings had spent many evenings at the base of the wooden monstrosity, which seven-year-old Eloise had christened Argus. When asked by their father why she'd chosen the name, she'd shrugged and said that, as the many-eyed giant Argus was all-seeing, it was only fitting that their father's all-seeing device share the name. No one had been able to argue the point, although her father still referred to it as his flying pig, for reasons none of them quite understood.

Aster huddled in her woolen cloak and watched the lowering sun brush the edge of the sky in orange and purple. It had always been her favorite part of the day—the in-between moments when the sun yielded the heavens to the moon and stars. She adjusted the wool wrap higher on her neck and willed her hands not to freeze in her gloves. So far, they were not heeding her silent commands. She'd just resigned herself to returning to the manor when a sound behind her caused her to turn.

Andrew.

"I thought I might find you here," he said. "I remember how much you enjoy this time of day, especially from the Hill."

She nodded, insomuch as her wrappings allowed. He sat next to her on Argus's wooden platform, his shoulder brushing hers, and withdrew a linen bundle from his pocket.

Her brows dipped at the clinking sound of broken glass. He unwrapped the linen, and she saw the watch she'd purchased for him. Her lips tilted in a sad smile.

"It's the gift I wrote to you about—the one meant as an encouragement for your safe return."

He frowned and ran a finger over the engraving on the lid. "You didn't write to me about this."

"Yes," she said, "I did. It was in the same letter when I asked you . . . when I asked if you still had an affection for me." Despite her attempts otherwise, the words came out as a mere whisper.

He stared at her, brows tipped in a steep V, before taking both of her hands in his. The watch lid was cold, its bent edges rough beneath their hands.

"Aster, I never received that letter. If I had—" He stopped and swallowed.

"But you replied," she said. "You wrote back and told me about the general's ball."

His frown was a mixture of confusion and affront. "You asked me if I held you in affection, and you thought I responded with a tale about curry?"

Her heart tripped at his words, but they still didn't explain why he'd remained in India after leaving the army. *Don't retreat from the conclusion.*

"It's come to my attention," she said, "that I've not been looking at things rationally."

"You haven't?"

"No." She pulled her hand from his and stood to pace before him. "The most elemental requirement of a successful mathematical proof is to assemble all the facts and only then follow the logic to a conclusion."

He blinked.

"I don't think I have all the facts," she whispered.

"What—what facts are you lacking?"

"Why did you come to England, Andrew? Why *now*?"

He stretched his legs, his hand rubbing absently at his thigh. She stopped pacing and stood before him. Her foot itched to tap, but she held it still and waited. And waited.

"The short answer," he began, "is that your sister wrote to me."

"Eloise?"

"Helen."

Aster frowned. "And the long answer?"

"Helen informed me of your betrothal. I—I couldn't let you marry anyone else."

"You came back to England—you traveled months across oceans—because you learned I was betrothed?"

"Yes."

"Why?"

He sighed in exasperation. "Because I love you. Because you're the only one who will ever make my heart sing."

She inhaled deeply, and the cold air burned her lungs. The sky had darkened, and the sun's colors were more vibrant than they'd been moments before. But, she supposed, that could have just been the joy in her heart.

"I should tell you," she said, "that before I left London, Mr. Church and I decided we don't suit. He—he doesn't make my heart sing." Her smile was watery as she confessed.

He took her hand and pulled her back down to the platform next to him.

"If you love me," she said, "why did you stay away for so long, even after you left the army?"

He studied the tips of his boots then turned back to her. "I went away to make something of myself."

She frowned and started to interrupt, but he wouldn't permit it. "I know you don't suffer idleness, Aster. Mediocrity. If we'd married seven years ago, I'd have been a disappointment to you. To me. I wanted to be sure I was enough for you."

"You foolish, ridiculous—I never wanted you to be any more than what you are. I only wanted *you*."

"You may not have wanted more, but you *deserve* it. And I wanted to be that for you. I want to be *more*. And to be honest, I was a coward, afraid of disappointing you. And myself."

Her breath—the air that had burned her lungs moments before, froze in her chest as tears flooded her eyes. She blinked them back. "I love you, too," she whispered.

He reached for her, and she settled in the curve of his arm. "We're a pair, aren't we?" he said.

She sniffed and nodded then turned up at him. "Will you tell me about your injury?"

"There's not much to—"

"Andrew," she said softly but firmly. "I've seen how you limp at times. I want to know all of you. That means even the difficult and unamusing parts. Allow me to know—to love—all of you."

He nodded, and she leaned her head on his shoulder as he told his tale. His words were halting at first, then his voice grew more certain. Tears burned her eyes—for his pain, for his months of recovery so far from home, for the loss of his captaincy. Relief soothed her as he told of his friend Montgomery Doyle's support. Then her hand held his as he shared his despondency, how at times he'd thought death would have been preferable to the pain, how he'd suffered under the weight of guilt for bemoaning his good fortune in surviving.

She smiled as he told her how he'd boldly tossed his ebony cane to an elderly man at the port in Bombay, determined to return to England without it. He'd walked the ship's deck for hours at a time until he was weak with fatigue, just to strengthen his leg.

"You are the bravest man I know," she said softly. "And the most stubborn." Then, as he began to refute her, she added, "I think you have a good friend in Montgomery Doyle, and a man's friends say much of his character. You wouldn't question his—or my—judgment, would you?"

His arm tightened around her. "Never," he agreed.

"What will you do now?"

His chest expanded as he drew a large breath. "I intend to remain in London, with you." At her waiting silence, he added, "Do you remember when I told you about the filigree?"

She nodded uncertainly.

He reached into a pocket of his vest and retrieved a small leather pouch. He untied the string and withdrew a small object before turning to her.

"I've made a small fortune designing and trading jewelry. I've partnered with a gentleman in Bombay—a local jeweler who's instructed me in the old ways—and we mean to expand our reach to England. I had a lot of time on my hands while my leg healed, and I've spent the past months perfecting this ring. It's not as dear as the woven bit of twisted weeds you carry about in your book"— her brows dipped at that—"but I hope you'll accept it as a sign of my love for you. I hope you'll allow me the honor of being your husband."

He held the ring to her and she took it. It was crafted of fine gold threads woven together in an impossibly delicate pattern. At the center was a brilliant white stone surrounded by small diamonds. The gems caught the sun's final golden rays as it dipped below the horizon.

"It's a moonstone," he explained. "The moon, to go with my wondrous star. If you'll have me, that is."

She sniffed and smiled. "Yes! Of course, yes!"

His green eyes glowed impossibly bright, and he pressed his lips to hers, cradling her cheek with one hand and warming them both as he breathed her in. His lips were soft and firm and perfectly shaped to hers. She wondered if she would ever need the stars in the heavens when he had the power to spark them behind her eyelids.

When he finally pulled away, he slowly removed her glove. Lifting her shaking hand, he slid the ring onto her finger as the first stars began winking in the sky. The action was so reminiscent of the day seven years before, when he'd slid a band of twisted weeds onto her hand, that she nearly wept.

"But we're not married yet," she said.

"Aster, we're as good as," he said. And then he lifted her hand in his to point out their star's first glimmer.

EPILOGUE

ASTER PULLED HER WRAP TIGHTER against the cold
and wished she'd thought to don an extra pair of
woolen stockings. The floors of Redstone Hall were
not meant for traipsing about unshod. As she was
closer to her destination than to the bedchamber she
shared with Andrew, she pushed on, walking on
light toes until she reached the morning room.
Slowly, she peered around the door post until she
spied her quarry.

Her parents. Her father dipped his head toward
her mother, whispering something in her ear. Aster
felt only the tiniest bit of guilt for spying on them.

The warm, spicy scent at her back alerted her to
Andrew's presence. She turned to him with one

finger at her lips. He quirked a single brow at her but remained silent, turning his attention to the scene in the morning room.

They'd just that day returned to Redstone Hall from their home in London. They'd passed a noisy but enjoyable evening with Aster's family, and tomorrow they would visit Fernwood. Her husband had not retired for the night as he'd been reviewing a new import contract, but he wore a warm dressing gown over his lawn shirt and trousers. She glanced down to see his own stocking-clad toes curled against the cold.

She turned back to survey the morning room, delighted when her father began dropping coins and paper-wrapped sweets into the shoes lined before the room's great bow window. The slippers and boots were too large for a visit from St. Nicholas, but this time next year, there would be a smaller pair alongside hers and Andrew's.

Her husband's lips tickled her shoulder, and he lifted her braid to achieve better access as he trailed kisses along the back of her neck. She fluttered a hand at him, not sure if she meant to impede his progress or encourage him.

"Come to bed, love," he said.

"Shh. In a moment."

Andrew squeezed her waist gently and she squeaked, clapping a hand over her mouth. Her father stiffened, head tilted to one side. She waited breathlessly to see if they'd be caught out, but he never turned.

Andrew chuckled into her ear, the rogue, and the warm rumbling sent energy zipping through her. She clasped his hand to still his teasing as they watched her parents move down the line of shoes. When they reached Andrew's boots her father paused, hands on his hips. Then he strode to the fireplace and scooped something from the ash bin.

Andrew went still and asked, "What's he doing?"

Her mother's soft laugh reached them from the morning room, and Aster stifled her own giggle with her hand.

"Did he—did he just put coal in my boot?"

THE END

Thank you for reading! If you enjoyed this story, you might also enjoy these other titles featuring the Corbyn family:
The Astronomer's Obsession (Harry and Celeste)
Light of a Nile Moon (Helen Corbyn)
Stars of Twilight Fair (Edmund Corbyn)
Beneath a Brighton Sun (Eloise Corbyn)

Be the first to know when new titles are released! Subscribe for updates at klynsmithauthor.com and receive the sweet Regency novella, Discovering Wynne, as a gift!

AFTERWARD

I create a mood board of the visual references I use when writing. If you would like to see my inspiration for Andrew, Aster and their frosty environs, please check out my Pinterest board at https://www.pinterest.com/klynsmithauthor/star-of-wonder-klynsmithauthorcom/.

Star of Wonder is a book of fiction based on historical events and attitudes of the time. My writing process includes extensive research into the language, customs and technologies of the time, among other things. While many sources were instrumental in helping shape Aster and Andrew's story, I would like to especially recognize *Letters from India* by Victor Jacquemont.

This French botanist's account, published in 1834, inspired some of the details of Andrew's time in India, such as his cliffside accident and the youthful doctor with the unsteady hand. Sometimes truth really is stranger than fiction, and I'm grateful to historians like Jacquemont for providing such a rich field of inspiration.

For purposes of 19th century Victorian authenticity, I've opted for the British styling for the cities of

Mumbai (Bombay), Kanpur (Cawnpore) and Kolkata (Calcutta). This is in no way meant to minimize or ignore the complex effects of colonization on these rich and diverse regions.

BOOKS BY K. LYN SMITH

Something Wonderful
The Astronomer's Obsession
The Artist's Redemption
The Physician's Dilemma

Hearts of Cornwall
Discovering Wynne (Prequel Novella)
Jilting Jory
Matching Miss Moon
Kissing Kate
Saving Miss Swan
Charming the Captain
Engaging Miss Enderby*
Regarding Rebecca

Love's Journey
Star of Wonder
Light of a Nile Moon
Stars of Twilight Fair
Beneath a Brighton Sun

* Part of the Hearts in Bloom
Regency Anthology.
Visit klynsmithauthor.com for the
most up-to-date list of titles.

ABOUT THE AUTHOR

K. Lyn Smith writes sweet historical romance about ordinary people finding extraordinary love. Her debut novel, The Astronomer's Obsession, was a finalist for the National Excellence in Romantic Fiction Award, and many of her other titles have been shortlisted for honors such as the American Writing Award, the Carolyn Reader's Choice Award, the HOLT Medallion and the Maggie Award.

When she's not lost in the pages of a book, you can find her with family, traveling to far-off places and binging period dramas. And space documentaries. Weird, right?

Visit www.klynsmithauthor.com, where you can subscribe for new release updates and access to exclusive bonus content.